Graveyard Gold

Clay Gideon ranched the Lazy G spread in Bannister County. He was the last of the Johnny Rebs to hold title to land in this Yankee-dominated part of Colorado and although the Civil War was over you'd never know it by the way they treated Gideon.

And when Bull Blanchard got the notion that there was gold on Lazy G it was like starting the war all over again. This time it was Yankees against Gideon, an Indian and an old mountain man who didn't even have his own teeth . . . but he had a Sharps Big Fifty, Gideon had his Henry and the Indian his bow.

Would it be enough to take on the whole Yankee Reconstruction?

Graveyard Gold

HANK J. KIRBY

A Black Horse Western

ROBERT HALE · LONDON

© Hank J. Kirby 2005
First published in Great Britain 2005

ISBN 0 7090 7743 2

Robert Hale Limited
Clerkenwell House
Clerkenwell Green
London EC1R 0HT

Typeset by
Derek Doyle & Associates, Shaw Heath.
Printed and bound in Great Britain by
Antony Rowe Limited, Wiltshire

CHAPTER 1

BAD DAY FOR GIDEON

Standing on the boardwalk outside the depot to watch the stage roll out of Bannister Springs, Clay Gideon's jaw jutted like a cliff in the ruggedest part of the Moonlights.

He could see her light lavender dress at the window – this side closest to him, too – even see the golden hair beneath the cocked bonnet. But she had her hand up to the side of her face and did not wave or even look towards him. He sighed a little, though his face showed nothing, only its usual lean wolfishness, perhaps the tanned flesh across the high cheekbones stretched a little more taut than usual. His thumbs were hooked into his gun belt.

A man stepped out of the depot, lighting a cigar, flicking the spent vesta into the street. A metal star tugged at this man's shirt pocket and he squinted sun-seasoned eyes, spoke around the cigar clenched between his teeth,

'Another man down to feminine wiles.'

Gideon didn't look at him. 'We had a couple years – some of it good.'

'That's the part to remember. Not this.' The sheriff gestured to the retreating stage, almost obscured by grey dust now as it headed for the trail through the Moonlights.

When Gideon said nothing, only continued to stare after the swaying Concord, the lawman said a little testily:

'You ain't gonna tie one on!'

'Might have a drink or two, Abe.'

Abe Chance straightened, those middle-aged eyes hard and chilling fast.

'Like to be able to count on that – one or two.'

Gideon shrugged his wide shoulders.He was average height, which made him 'tall' in this town, but he didn't swagger or throw his muscular weight around. He was mostly a quiet *hombre* but these last few months when his wife, Lanie, had started her endless complaints about the kind of life they lived out here, he had thrown one or two drunks and had turned out to be surprisingly aggressive. He still owed Joel Eastman some money for repairs to a bar mirror in O'Bannion's Razzle Dazzle saloon.

'Clay, you behave. That's all I gotta say.'

It was more than Gideon had to say by way of reply. He heaved off the depot porch-post with a wrench of one shoulder, tilted his sweat-stained curlbrim over his eyes a little and crossed the street towards the saloon.

Sheriff Abel Chance sighed, set his own hat square on his head and took his cigar from his mouth to spit. He shook his head as he watched Gideon push through the batwings, then ambled back along the walk towards his office.

He figured he would be seeing Gideon again this afternoon before long.

He was right. But, actually, it was almost full dark before O'Bannion sent a runner to get the sheriff and tell him that Clay Gideon and Bo Flynn were tearing up the Razzle Dazzle bar at a tornado rate.

It happened this way:

Gideon was more sad than he allowed to show; the end of a marriage, even a fiery one, was nothing to set the blood afizzing. Lanie had been a good enough woman, simply wasn't cut out for his kind of lone-ranch living at the foot of a mountain range in a town that had had hell kicked out of it by both sides in the War. It was hard living in a Southern state after the War. Especially hard if it was your home state. He should never have brought Lanie out here but he had seen the land, knew enough about topography and soil to see a potential here – especially as the Moonlights were swarming with mavericks that had run wild all through the long bloody years.

His enthusiasm had fired Lanie eventually and she had turned her back on a decent home, gradually rebuilding, back in Georgia, and come to live in south-west Colorado with Gideon. He had nurtured her slowly, gently, thought he was having considerable success, but after she lost the baby – well, Lanie changed, and he couldn't blame her. She'd almost died because they were so far from good medical aid. She was convinced that the baby could have been saved if they had had easier access to a decent hospital. It had been all downhill from that time on – finishing here, this afternoon, almost two years to the day since their marriage.

Yeah – sad thing. Lanie seemed cool, cold, glad to get away. No squabble over the ranch – she wanted nothing from him, left him a legacy that was a mix of sweet memories and bitterness.

Time to wash the taste of that part of his life out of his throat and move right along – to where he didn't know.

He was thinking about it, staring into a glass of rotgut – his fifth, sixth, tenth? Didn't matter – at a corner table when he heard a voice say:

'Man don't take care of his woman's needs he has to expect 'em to walk out. Now me, if she'd been my wife, with them looks and that golden hair – man, I can feel it now, runnin' like silk through my fingers!' A bottle-neck clinked against a glass rim. 'Yessir, I'd've made sure she wouldn't't've *wanted* to leave me.'

'Easy, Bo!' another voice said with an edge of worry. 'He'll hear.'

'So he can hear. Free country now we won the War. I'll say what I like, where 'n' when I like – and no damn Reb is gonna tell me different.'

Gideon lifted his gaze then. Bo Flynn, big, husky, was a man who enjoyed a fight and had done more than his share of helping the Razzle Dazzle to lose

8

some of its dazzle over the years since he had been working for Bull Blanchard, Gideon's neighbour on the Graveyard spread.

Bo had a chopped-up face but there was a certain look to it that intrigued some women and he had a reputation with the ladies of Bannister Springs. It was said a marriage band was no barrier to his desires. Now he looked directly at Gideon with those clear blue eyes and lifted his shotglass in a kind of mocking salute. He raised his voice.

'Just sayin', too bad your wife run out, Reb – I coulda looked after her if you din' have the energy – or the wherewithal.'

His two companion riders from Blanchard's, Ed Bragg and Cheadle, chuckled. Gideon didn't. He had been drinking ever since the stage had left, had had nothing to eat. He was at a low ebb: too many things were going wrong lately. He'd had a bad day and Bo Flynn was doing his best to make it worse.

So Clay Gideon downed his drink, stood, hitched at his belt and rubbed the back of his hand across his nostrils, never taking his grey-green eyes off Flynn.

Then, with two strides, he covered the distance between them and his right fist exploded in the middle of Bo's face. His left hand snatched at Flynn's belt, yanked him forward and spun the big ramrod, hit him on the back of his neck and drove his forehead into the zinc edge of the bar.

Three seconds after Flynn had stopped speaking, he was writhing on the floor, his face and mouth a mask of blood. Gideon was standing over him, waiting for him to either pass out or get to his feet. . . .

9

Bragg, chunky, a brawler and beetle-browed, said 'Hey!' and reached for Gideon. His groping hand found only air, until the bottle Gideon snatched off the counter smashed across his wrist. There was a tolerably loud crack and Bragg sagged in the middle, stumbled down the bar, trying to stifle a sob of pain. Cheadle, lanky, rawboned, hesitated, started to reach for his six-gun but Gideon tossed the bottle at him and the man instinctively tried to catch it. The rancher stepped in and pounded his midriff, picked him up bodily and slammed him down on top of Bo Flynn, who was groggily trying to stagger upright.

Both men went down in a tangled heap.

By then, O'Bannion's runner was well on the way to the law office and by the time Abe Chance came lumbering in, holding his sawed-off hickory pickaxe handle, the bar was a shambles.

Gideon and Flynn were slugging it out toe to toe, overturning tables and chairs; yelling men were leaping out of the way, cursing the fighters. Clothes ripped and the dark stains of sweat changed to the redder stains of fresh blood. Flynn teetered but managed to whip his big head to the left so that Gideon's fist skidded across his neck. It hurt and made him cough but he managed to stay in a fairly solid stance, ducked under and put a gnarled fist just above Gideon's belt.

Clay's legs trembled and he sagged. Flynn's beefy shoulder hooked him under the jaw, knuckles pounding at the lean, hard-muscled midriff. Gideon's back hit the zinc edge of the bar and sickening pain shot through his spine and kidneys. His face went grey and

Bo, sensing victory here, took one long step forward, right fist cocked way back past his head.

Gideon seemed slow to move out of the way as the fist flashed forward – but he wasn't there when the blow should have landed and put his nose somewhere towards the back of his head. He had ducked low, dropped to one knee, now came up with a roar of straining strength. He buried a hand in Bo's crutch, jammed the heel of his other hand up under the man's jutting jaw and lifted, roaring like a lion on the African veld. The sound Bo Flynn made was higher-pitched and feeble in comparison. But then Gideon spun and with that heavy ramrod suspended above his head, iron-knotted arms atremble, he bared his teeth and hurled Bo over the bar.

Even as he did so, he felt his belly sink: *Oh, no! Not the mirror again!*

Yes, the mirror. Bo's boots hit first and the smoky glass, still patched with sticky tape from the last time Gideon had brawled in here, shattered musically.

Clay Gideon leaned his aching arms on the edge of the bar, gasping, head hanging between his shaking arms, and lifted his gaze slowly. There was a triangular shard still jammed in the frame and he caught a glimpse of his blood-streaked, swollen face, one eye almost closed, a tooth through his bottom lip, thick blood oozing from his nostrils and dripping off his chin.

Then something blurred into the reflection and his mind just recognized it for an instant before the hickory handle smashed across his skull and suddenly the world was a dark, empty place.

*

They called him Old Buckskin, but he only wore trousers made of that material these days, not the full outfit he used to have when scouting for the Rebs during the War or trapping in the snow-locked Rockies.

He stared through the bars of Gideon's cell and waited patiently for the battered man – now painted with acryflavine and iodine, a tape across split knuck-les on his left hand – to come round. It was dark outside and light from the jail corridor lantern washed only into part of the cell.

Eventually, Gideon sensed the old scout. He opened his one good eye, grunted and gradually worked his way to a sitting position.

'Time'zit?'

'Don't matter – Renny's gone.'

Gideon blinked, trying to absorb the words through the pounding in his skull. Renny was a cowhand who worked the spread with Old Buckskin, a young, cocky ranny who was pretty good with a rope.

'Gone? You mean quit?'

'I mean stole.' Buckskin's face looked kind of collapsed in on itself, not helped by the fact that he never wore his hand-carved deer-bone teeth unless he was eating. And then not always.

Gideon blinked, wincing because the movement hurt his face. 'What. . . ?'

'Blanchard. Come ridin' in at supper time. Said he was expandin' the Graveyard and would be takin''

GRAVEYARD GOLD

over our Lazy G – north-west pasture, anyways, but he
was willin' to take the lot if you wanted to get rid of it.'

It took Gideon some time to absorb this. He
squinted.

'Offered Renny and me double what you pay.
Since you don't pay me nothin', it was no deal for
me. Renny liked the idea of an extra twenty, though.'

'He went to work for Bull?'

'Uh-huh. Moved right on out.'

'What gave Blanchard the idea I wanted to sell?
Just because Lanie up and left?'

'I'd say so. Plus you been havin' some bad luck
lately, what with them mavericks bustin' outta the
holdin' canyon, the brush fire on the east slopes
that's left us short of grass. . . .'

Gideon lifted a sore, aching hand. 'I know what's
happened.' He frowned. 'Bull Blanchard suddenly
wants to expand – into my place. And when he first
came here, after he found Lazy G was already taken,
I recollect him saying the only way he could go then
was south-east, back into the Moonlights, when he
had enough cows to run the slopes. What happened
when you didn't take his offer?'

'Told me to light out – there wouldn't be a place
for me here.'

Gideon limped across to the bars, puzzled:

'He figures he's moving in right away? Son of a
bitch hasn't even come in to make me an offer!'

'Kind of figures this time you're gonna be on Abe
Chance's chain-gang for quite a spell. Bo's all busted
up and O'Bannion's screamin' like an Apache about
his mirror again.'

Gideon groped his way back to the bunk and eased down on to it. 'Yeah,' he said heavily. 'But why's Bull interested in that north-west pasture? There's nothing much there, 'cept part of the grave where those Dutchies were massacred just at the end of the War. You found a few of their bones on our side . . .'

'That's why there's thick patches of grass there. Bodies make good fertilizer.'

Clay Gideon couldn't think. This was beyond him right now.

But he knew, somehow, that it was mighty impor- tant – and to take care of it, he had to get out of here.

CHAPTER 2

BURNT OUT

Renny was a mite afraid of Bull Blanchard. Not that Bull was too frightening in appearance, but there was a certain twist to his thick lips and something that spoke of death in the back of his grey eyes. He was a big man, of course, not particularly tall but thick through like a mountain cedar. He intimidated most men.

He sat on his ranch porch now as Renny slouched up to the foot of the steps, escorted by the wrangler, Peewee.

Renny shuffled his feet as he waited for Blanchard to speak. There had to be something scary about a man who called his spread 'The Graveyard' and used a tombstone with a crude cross for a brand.

Bull spun away the stub of a cigar, just missing Renny's head, and slouched down in his chair.

'Gonna take my offer, huh?'

'Yessir, Mr Blanchard, I can sure use the money.

15

Clay's OK but he's short of cash.'

'If I'm paying you double, you'll work for it.'

'Fine with me,' Renny assured him, smiling with his large teeth, a little spittle showing on the breadth of gum he displayed.

'You stand back from me when you talk to me, you got a mouth like that,' Blanchard said without expression and, although Renny was already six or seven feet away, the cowboy stepped back. 'Gideon's wife get away?'

'I guess. Me an' Buckskin never went to see her off.'

'Buckskin – that old fool still on the spread?'

Renny shook his head. 'Went in to see Clay. About you offerin' us more pay, I guess.'

Bull glanced at Peewee. 'Where's Bo?'

'Town.'

Blanchard's thick lips compressed a little. 'He prodding Gideon again?' Peewee shrugged and Bull glared briefly. 'OK. Tell Coke I want to see him and . . .'

Bragg rode in just then, Cheadle behind, some hundred yards back. Blanchard stood and leaned on the rail, waiting, watching the bruised men approach.

'Bo done it again. Riled Gideon an' got tossed through the mirror in the Razzle Dazzle,' Bragg announced.

'Gideon must've been feeling pretty good, by the looks of you two. Chance lock him up?'

'Yeah. Bo'll be back tomorrer. Doc wants to check his shoulder or somethin'.'

16

Blanchard took his time about taking a fresh cigar from his leather case inside his jacket pocket. He lit up, watching the others.

'Gideon's locked up. How about that Buckskin?'

'Still in town, I reckon.'

'Lazy G's deserted, then.'

No one said anything.

Bull Blanchard drew deeply on his cigar. 'Go have your supper boys. Then come see me.' He suddenly smiled. 'Could be Clay Gideon's gonna have a bad night as well as a bad day. . . .'

Abe Chance was in no mood for compromise the next morning and he passed on his sourness to Judge Galbally.

'Yessir, Judge, it's Clay Gideon again. I warned him not to get drunk and start trouble but he never took no notice and now he's busted up the Razzle's bar mirror again, put Bo Flynn in Doc McClements' infirmary and is in a right cussin' mood this mornin'.'

Galbally, thick silver hair standing out from his head like wire, curled a lip under his drooping moustache and glared at Gideon where he stood in the dock, battered face a mess of blotches in the dim light of the courtroom. There was no gallery of spectators: this was a closed court and if Gideon had been feeling better no doubt he would have realized something was scheduled to happen here – not necessarily in his best interests.

It had worked before, with Carmichael and Skene, the only other two Rebs who had settled out here. They were gone now. . . .

17

'Got anything to say, Mr Gideon?'

'Guess I'm sorry, Judge. Didn't mean to let things get outta hand but – well, Bo Flynn's got a bad mouth and he started in about my wife and – I've had a bellyful of bad luck lately, Judge! I'm beat down lower than I ever remember and I guess I went off the deep end.'

'You did. Pay all damages. Give you seven days. Or you can have three months on the chain-gang to work it off.'

'Judas wept! Three months! Hell, I only got Old Buckskin to take care of the ranch now! They tell me Bull Blanchard wants to buy my spread or part of it or something but I haven't had time to even consider his offer—'

'Then you get considering, son. I don't aim to tolerate this kinda thing. You Johnny Rebs got to get used to the fact that you lost the War and now it's time to follow the rules – Yankee rules. You've kicked over the traces before this and I've been lenient, but leniency's at an end. You been thumbing your nose too often in our direction. . . .' The judge glanced at Chance. 'You better let him go back to his spread for a week and see if he can raise the money somehow, Abe.'

Chance wasn't too happy about that but agreed. Then, before Gideon could step down steeply from the dock, the courtroom door opened and Bull Blanchard came in, right on cue, followed by his trouble-buster, Coke, Renny, and, trailing them all, the gangling, shambling form of Old Buckskin.

The old scout kept himself separate from the others.

Blanchard made his apologies to the court, asked for and got permission from the judge to talk to Clay Gideon.

'Clay, I got some bad news for you. I mean, I guess you got enough on your plate right now but – fact is you've had a fire out at Lazy G.'

Gideon stiffened, frowning at Blanchard, too stunned to speak right up.

'A – fire. . . ?' He managed eventually and Bull gestured to Buckskin.

'Ask the oldster.'

Buckskin nodded to Gideon. 'All over by the time I got back, Clay. Barn, corrals, cabin, all gone.'

'How the hell. . . ?' Gideon glanced at Renny but the young cowboy avoided his gaze, picked at some ash and smears of carbon on his hands. He seemed mighty uneasy, like he wished he were somewhere else.

Buckskin opened his gummy mouth to speak but Bull Blanchard somehow managed to look kind of embarrassed and even shuffled his big feet a little.

'Judge,' he siad, 'I guess I gotta take the blame.' All eyes turned to the big-set rancher. It wasn't often anyone heard Blanchard use that contrite tone. 'We were burning a firebreak yest'y afternoon . . . I aim to plant alfalfa in a field across the narrow part of the creek from Clay's place and I figured with summer starting to warm up, I best take precautions so I didn't lose it to a brush fire.' He looked around help-lessly and shrugged. 'Burn-back went well enough but . . . I guess there must've been some sparks left and . . . we had a wind out there last night that

19

would've blown the hair outta your scalp. Guess some of the sparks found their way across into Clay's barn where he had his hay. . . .'

Gideon swore softly under his breath: could he really be that unlucky? Well, with all the other jinxed things that had happened to him lately, he reckoned he could. He squared up to Blanchard.

'How much is left?'

'Lots of charcoal, and that's about it. Sorry, Clay.'

Gideon seemed to deflate.

'Well, too bad you didn't make an offer earlier to buy me out, Bull.'

'Aw, been thinking about it for some time, but – look, I'll still make you an offer, Clay. Hell, I already admitted it's my fault, or the fault of some of my men. I feel bad about it. I was mainly interested in the north-east pasture, but seeing as you're wiped out – well, reckon it's only fair that I take the lot off your hands.' He paused a moment then said slowly: 'I know it ain't really the right thing to say, but now your wife's left and . . . all this has happened . . . well, it could even be seen as a stroke of luck for you.'

Gideon's bruised stare was hard to read, but there was no sign of friendliness on his battered face as he looked at his neighbour.

'Depends on where you're standing,' he said heavily. 'I'll need time to think this over, Bull.'

'Sure, that's OK—'

'No.'

They all looked up sharply as Judge Galbally dropped the single word into the dim room.

'Clay, this is your only way out of a lot of trouble.

Bull's got the answer whether he intended it to be so or not. You take his offer and clear your debts. Then you can leave town with a clean slate and make a new start elsewhere.'

The words rang dimly in the quiet that followed. All eyes settled on Gideon. He was silent for a long time, then raised his gaze to the judge after sweeping it across Blanchard and Sheriff Chance.

'I'll think it over,' he said flatly.

The gavel exploding on its desk-base made Renny and a couple of others jump. Galbally hunched forward across his desk.

'You will make your deal with Bull Blanchard before you leave this court, or you will leave it in leg-irons. Now, what'll be?'

Gideon looked at them all one by one. Slowly he nodded gently.

'Should've seen it coming,' he said quietly. 'All the troubles, all the so-called bad luck over the months – the treatment of Lanie, delaying her mail orders, losing her letters home, misplacing her things, drunks going out of their way to upset her – things getting worse for her, every day, in every way. Lazy G's the only spread still run by a Johnny Reb in this part of the country. Been a thorn in your sides all that time, ain't it? And here I was figuring I'd stick no matter what, because I had no money to move anywhere else – and no one seemed remotely interested in Lazy G. But you were just biding your time, too, weren't you? All of you.' He made his contempt clear for them all to see. 'And at last it's all come together for you. You've got your chance to wipe me

21

out, pile up debts I can't hope to meet, till now I have the choice of taking Bull's offer or spending months on the chain gang.'

'With nothin' to come back to,' Coke said slowly, a hard-faced man of only medium stature but with the tightest unsmiling mouth this side of the Painted Desert; a man who liked to point out the obvious. 'Know what I'd do.'

'Don't sound very grateful, do he, Judge?' allowed Sheriff Chance. There was a mocking light in his eyes that was reflected in Galbally's rheumy orbs. 'I mean – we're tryin' to give him a break, but . . .' He shook his head, shrugging.

Obviously Gideon was a lost cause in the lawman's opinion.

Gideon nodded. 'Yeah. No place to go, nothing to look forward to. Good old Yankee know-how, eh? Take your time, work towards what you want and sooner or later you'll find a way to break the Johnny Reb. . . .'

'I'd say we broke you,' Coke sneered.

Then Galbally smashed the gavel down again. 'What's your decision, Gideon? I'll make this an official ruling of the court if you want, but I'll have your decision right now!'

Gideon's glare made the silver-haired man flinch but the rancher settled his gaze on Bull Blanchard.

'What's your offer, Bull?'

Blanchard smiled. 'I think you'll find it fair. . . .'

The Indian's big, horny splay feet slipped on the black ooze so he was forced to drop his end of the swamp-sodden dead tree. Muck splattered over the ragged bottoms of his trousers but was hardly noticeable amongst the other stains.

Dollops of stinking ooze slapped against Gideon's naked torso but he scooped them off one by one with his already muddy hands. The Indian's angular face was watching him closely and the man nodded very slightly by way of apology.

'You shoulda took Bull's offer, Gideon. Least you wouldn't be bustin' your back in this stinkhole.'

Gideon stooped and locked his hands around his end of the log again. 'Ready?'

The Indian grunted and picked up the slippery tree trunk. They slogged awkwardly up the muddy slope, slipping and sliding, wrenching muscles, cursing silently, not wasting their breath doing it out loud.

The nearest guard was watching boredly but there was nothing bored about the way he held his Spencer rifle. If they dropped the log again, one of them would feel the iron butt of the small but deadly rifle across the back of his head. If any of the other prisoners on the chain-gang working this part of the swamp decided to take advantage of the diversion and make a run for it – well, so far no one Gideon knew had had speed enough to outrun a bullet.

'They say you can get outta here, all you gotta do is take Bull's offer.'

'That what they say?' murmured Gideon. He had been here three weeks now and was already a master at speaking without moving his lips, even looking as if he was totally uninterested in oral communication.

They dumped the log on top of several others, sliding it down between stakes already driven deep into the mud. The filthy swamp-water was beginning to back up against the crude dam wall. Soon the sheriff's wife would be able to tap into the pool it was forming, so she could have the convicts water her vegetable- and flower-patches.

'Why Bull want your place?'

Busying themselves washing off the thick layers of mud in the gurgling black water, Gideon didn't even glance at the Indian.

'Dunno. Guess they don't like Rebs, want rid of me.'

'Like Navajo, eh? Someone push, you push back.'

Gideon worked on and he and the Indian went back to where some of the other men were just finishing trimming the next tree to be laid in the rising dam wall.

He had thought about it often enough since Galbally had ordered him to be put in leg-irons and transferred to the chain-gang to serve his three months' sentence. He gave up when he couldn't come up with a good reason, other than that they simply wanted him out of this neck of the woods because he was a Southerner and they wanted to keep this area exclusively for genuine Yankees and their families.

It had happened in other places, he'd heard.

Bannister Springs was actually named after some Yankee colonel who had supervised the total annihilation of several defenceless Southern families, from Missouri to Texas, during his war exploits. It was his way of warning others not to shelter Rebels on the run. *See what can happen if you do.* These were easy targets, and the warnings were effective. But Bannister had been shot dead by a mystery woman not long ago, just before he could enjoy the full fruits of his labours. Some said it was his mistress.

She was never caught.

It was likely that Galbally, who was reconstrruction administrator as well as judge, had figured the newly formed Bannister County should not be contaminated by any Southerner. It was OK if they worked the spreads for the Yankee owners or did the donkey chores, but as for owning land . . . A resounding No!

Gideon had come through this country on the retreat south, liked what he saw, and when he was captured in St Louis at war's end, he had been detailed to work in a Lands Office. Here he found a survey map of south-west Colorado, and could easily pick out the land he had admired weeks earlier. On impulse, and for the trade of a jug of Southern Belle rotgut, a sergeant from Indiana had given him genuine papers, with the land registered in his name.

That deed had passed through all the intricate legal channels of the time – there was mostly chaos, which was how it went through so easily – but it ended up being one of the most solidly registered deeds outside of Washington itself.

Galbally and his crew must have found it a good deal harder to ride roughshod over him than they had Carmichael or Skene, who had only claimed a few acres at the Bannister Springs Lands Office . . . which came under Galbally's jurisdiction.

That must be it. They couldn't find a legal loop-hole they could use to kick him off and take over, so now they were going to destroy him.

But, although he was mostly apathetic, he wasn't dumb, and Clay Gideon sensed there was some deeper reason for Blanchard and the others wanting his land than just ridding the county of the last Johnny Reb.

While he was on the chain-gang they could use his land however they wanted and there was nothing he could do about it, but whatever they did would be illegal, simply because Lazy G was still solidly regis-tered to him.

He had heard a whisper that when Blanchard moved into the area and tried to claim the land, by then the Lazy G, he had literally kicked a Conestoga wagon apart in his anger when he learned it was already owned by a Johnny Reb, registered in St Louis to boot. Others claimed he had merely shrugged and said he would expand in the other direction, didn't matter a hill of beans to him.

But Gideon knew now – he *knew*, even though he didn't have any proof – that Blanchard desperately wanted title to Lazy G. That's why he was certain sure that they weren't going to simply let him serve his three months, then turn him loose, and make him another – better? – offer. Bull Blanchard had already approached him twice, upping the first offer, and when that hadn't worked, Bull had hinted he could use his influence with Galbally to have his sentence reduced.

Gideon had simply walked away back to the chain-gang each time.

Now, as they prepared to carry another tree across the swamp, the Indian said quietly:

'Heard somethin' else about you.'

Gideon waited but he had had a sense of foreboding this past week and he wondered if the Navajo was going to confirm that black emptiness that had been gnawing at his belly and give him more bad news.

He saw the lice in the Indian's coal-black hair as the man bent across in front of him to get a better grip on the tree.

'You never gonna leave the chain gang – only in a turpentine sack.'

These were the large hessian sacks used for carrying turpentine bark. They kept a big pile behind the tool shed. They were also used for disposing of corpses, which were sewn up in the bags and dumped in the middle of the swamp where they disappeared for ever into the primeval slop.

CHAPTER 3

ONLY WAY OUT

He had been expecting something to happen to him every day since Chance had brought him out to the chain-gang camp. It had been rough, but no rougher than what most newcomers could expect from a band of hard *hombres,* some of whom were serving sentences they didn't deserve.

But the real trouble started the very night after the Indian had warned him: it was clear enough to Gideon. They had decided that the only way they could get their hands on his land was to put him out of the way permanently.

So he was alert when the lights-out whistle blew and the dormitory hut was plunged into darkness. But he wasn't expecting the bunk to collapse.

The bunks were double-tiered. A man named Acuff was above Gideon. He was a fat man, coming in at 200 pounds, played the banjo, had been unable to pay the fine for stealing a chicken. That little caper had earned him a month on Chance's chain-gang. He said little, worried a lot about his wife and child in Denver. He was pretty dumb and Gideon never did blame him for what happened.

Gideon was settling back on the lower bunk. He froze when he heard a distinct creaking, then the unmistakable cracking of wood fibres. He rolled quickly over the side board and sprawled on the floor on all fours. A single moment later, Acuff's huge body smashed down on to Gideon's bunk, splintered the warped planks and crashed on through to the floor. The big man grunted, fat arms hanging over the shattered bunk-frame, dazed, hurt and moaning.

Lanterns were burning in an instant and the hut guard together with two more heavy-set outside men clutching long hickory billies, charged in.

They made straight for Gideon's corner and he knew right then this had been a set-up for sure: the start of their campaign to get him.

It was stupid the way they twisted it around, without logic, reciting by rote, accusing him of partly sawing through the bunk uprights so Acuff would crash down.

'On top of me?' Gideon asked, earning a brittle look from the head guard, a beefy man named Hustler.

'You weren't in that bunk when he come crashin' down,' Hustler growled.

'Only because I heard the uprights giving way. . . .'

Hustler thrust his face to within a couple of inches of Gideon's.

'*Only because you was expectin' it and got outta there*

pronto!' he shouted.

'Why the hell would I want Acuff to fall? What could I gain from a fool move like that?'

'How the hell would I know! Are you back-answerin' me, Reb.' Hustler displayed crooked, stained teeth in a tight grin and Gideon knew he had walked right into the trap.

They didn't give a damn about Acuff, who looked as if he had sustained a broken collar-bone and some sort of back injury, or anything else to do with the incident. The thing had been set to prod Gideon into an unwise reaction to more bullying. Just that mild *Why the hell would I. . . ?* was all they needed.

The end of the hickory billy jabbed upward and Gideon stepped back instinctively. The blow missed and Hustler stumbled forward, an arm going out towards Gideon to steady him. Clay instinctively struck the arm aside and that was it.

The three of them moved in, hickory whistling through the air, rising and falling, thudding home again and again on Gideon's writhing body, until the writhing stopped. Then a brief tattoo from each man and Hustler led the way out, the other two guards dragging the bloody and unconscious Gideon between them.

The other prisoners watched in silence.

Gideon spent four days in solitary, a small, cramped sheet-iron cube out in the middle of the yard, well away from the three huts and the shade of any of the sparse trees. No room to stand, no room to even straighten out cramped legs. And no food or water – or toilet arrangements.

Abe Chance was there when they opened up and prodded him through a series of holes until he crawled out, filthy, weak, squinting. Chance stood above him as Gideon rested on hands and knees, gasping.

'Judge has given you another three months for your stupid shenanigans, Gideon. I'm here to tell you, they're gonna be the hardest three months of your life.' He paused, then added: ' 'Less you make some – arrangement – about that land of yours. . . .'

Gideon turned his throbbing head up, one eye still half-closed and blackened. His neck was too stiff to look up at an angle that allowed him to see Chance's face. So he turned his head a little more – and vomited on the sheriff's polished boots and trousers.

A week later, they dragged him out of the cube again, straight to the swamp, and put him to work, allowing him only a drink of water, no food.

'Don't fight,' the Indian said without moving his lips. 'They're waitin' for that.'

Gideon grunted.

'They're gonna kill you.'

'Gonna . . . try.'

'What you gonna do?'

'It's OK. They won't kill me.'

'Make damn good try.'

And they did.

They put a new man named Puddler on the logs with him, sent the Indian down the slope to the weed detail.

31

Gideon watched Puddler warily. The man looked fresh and well-fed, carried a few scars around his eyes and his nose had a slant to windward. He had big hands, the knuckles scarred.

'The hell you lookin' at?' Puddler growled belligerently.

'Prizefighter?' Gideon asked and Puddler looked surprised . . . even pleased.

'Champeen of the Pennsylvania Seventh Miners a while back . . . You done some fightin'?'

'Not in a long time – for money, that is. In the army I fought for my squad – A-Troop, Colorado Volunteers.'

Puddler spat. 'Reb trash. You get beat?'

Gideon shook his head and Puddler straightened, interested now.

'Never?'

' "Never" means nothing. Only had less than a dozen challenges.'

'But you won 'em all? Musta been low-grade or I'd've heard of you.' He looked thoughtful, kind of straining. 'Gideon . . . Nope, woulda recollected, prissy name like that.' He was trying hard to provoke enough of a retort to have an excuse for taking a swing at Gideon.

'You want to grab that end of the log? Guards're watching us.'

Puddler snapped his head up. The hard-faced guard on the slope frowned at Puddler, jerked his head towards Gideon. Puddler, a mouth-breather because of his crooked nose, nodded and waited until Gideon had lifted his end of the log, then delib-

32

erately dropped his own end, pushing it forward at the same time, driving the rough wood into the other's belly.

Gideon sprawled, sliding in the muck. Puddler effortlessly heaved the log so that it skidded down the slope after Gideon, rolling over him, mashing him into the ooze.

'Get that man outta there!' snarled the guard. 'The hell you think you're doin', Gideon. This ain't playtime.'

Puddler lumbered down the slope, ready to do what he had been hired for now. He reached for Gideon but pushed his face under the muck deliberately. Held it there till the man began to writhe and choke, then hauled him upright, picked up the gagging rancher and hurled him down on to the more solid ground.

Gideon lay there, feeling as if he was dying while his lungs tried to cough up the filthy muck choking them as they fought for air. Puddler looked at the guard.

'He's fightin' me every time I try to help him up. You see him take a swing at me?'

'Fight back. You got my permission,' the guard said with a twisted smile.

Puddler grinned and some of the other prisoners paled; they knew what Puddler was going to do to Gideon now.

'Here's where you break your record, mister,' Puddler growled, half-laughing as he moved in on Gideon. 'Here's where you get beat – but *good*!'

The Indian, standing nearby, heard and he looked

around for something he could do to stop what he knew now was going to be cold-blooded murder.

Puddler had Gideon on his feet now, still coughing, swaying. A huge muddy fist doubled up and swung. It seemed to the watchers that Gideon's head was about to fly off his shoulders amidst a shower of mud and slush which exploded from his long, fouled hair. Puddler struck again and again and then Gideon, rising one more time, thrust a double handful of mud into the prize-fighter's face, filling his eyes, mouth and nose. The big man choked and lurched.

Gideon butted him under the jaw and as Puddler staggered back, the guard came pounding in, swinging the Spencer rifle butt at Gideon's head.

Suddenly he stopped dead for a split second, rifle poised, and then his body lifted violently and was hurled back several feet in an arm-flailing somersault.

Hard on this unexpected acrobatic display came the thunder of a heavy gunshot, rolling across the swamplands with almost physical force, a sound much heavier than the report of a Spencer.

Men instinctively dropped flat. The guards stood frozen. Someone shooting at *them* was a novel experience. And then the man closest to the water butt suddenly spun as if jerked around by a lariat, his rifle flying out to one side. His body was still in mid-air, twisting, when a third guard started in a clumsy run, thrust along by something that struck him between the shoulders with the power and force of a locomotive.

Next the water-butt exploded, staves splintering and silver jets erupting. There were only two guards still left alive and neither of them seemed interested in trying to do anything about this . . . this . . . *what?* Attack? So far as they could tell there had only been the five shots, all coming from a single rifle.

A buffalo-gun, the Indian decided, crouching by a log. He looked at Gideon, bleeding, dazed, down on one knee, his mild resistance having almost exhausted him after so long in solitary.

'*G-i-d-e-o-nnnnnnnn!*'

The word flew over the camp, like a voice from the sky. Just the name. No encouragement. No directions. Just Clay Gideon's name.

But his head was still ringing from the pounding given him by Puddler. His ribs creaked, his belly was sore from Puddler's fists and the thrusting log. He heard the voice clearly enough, knew who it was, started to crawl towards the brush beyond the swamp-water, half-blinded by mud and blood.

Then the Indian was rushing towards him, the big, square hands lifting him, straightening him long enough to drop a shoulder and heave the rancher over his back.

The strong Navajo legs began to pound down the slope, splashing knee-deep into the stinking water, which slowed him. One of the guards figured he had better stop this and rose to one knee, firing his Spencer, levering fast. Lead splashed beside the Indian, just missing one of Gideon's trailing hands.

Then the hidden buffalo-gun thundered again and the guard was flung away like a bundle of laundry. The remaining guard whimpered as he ran hell for leather out of the camp back towards towrds town.

'Here!'

The staggering Indian heard the call and swung left but he had hardly done so when the same voice called again, from the right and slightly behind. He grunted, changed direction again, but he knew whoever it was had fought Indians, knew a few tricks that would tie white men in knots.

There was no more encouragement now and the Indian, breathing hard by this time, even his thick legs beginning to tremble with his burden, forced his way through slush that was more than half mud. Brush whipped across his face, and Gideon's, too, making the semi-conscious man moan. Twice he saw snakes but although the reptiles rose threateningly they made no strikes at him as he floundered past.

The slope had steepened: he was drawing above the swamp now. He heard distant voices and shouting behind. And then the chilling baying of the hounds.

His big, throbbing heart almost stopped as a man wearing a fringed buckskin shirt and matching trousers, all stained and mellowed from wilderness living, stepped into his path. The Sharps Big Fifty casually covered him as the newcomer gestured to his left.

'Hosses in there. You've earned a ride, Indian.'

'Nice shootin'. You Old Buckskin?'

'Most comfortable material there is. Gideon all right?'

'He'll be OK.'

They mounted and were well on the way towards the Moonlights before the raging sheriff and his cut-throat posse had cleared the chain-gang swamp camp where all the remaining prisoners had been locked in their huts, leg-ironed to their bunk stanchions.

There were seven missing, runaways who had taken advantage of the fracas at the swamp camp. Chance had promised the ones he locked in the hut that none of them would eat until Gideon and the Indian were recaptured, but every man there still hoped that Gideon would make good his escape.

Gideon hadn't said much in the three days they had been hiding out in the cave that Buckskin had prepared, high in the Moonlights, well back amongst the tangled draws and canyons.

His injuries didn't bother him too much, though they had slowed him down some. Buckskin had had fresh clothes and even his guns waiting for him, including his bullet moulds and fresh, sealed tins of percussion caps for the cylinder nipples. Clay pointed to the new buckskin shirt.

'See you been busy.'

Buckskin, long hair pulled back in a cue and tied with rawhide, squatted.

'Kept myself amused. Had me a feelin' you weren't gonna be allowed to serve out your sentence. Got a few things ready for your break. Courtesy Bannister general store, mostly.'

'I hadn't even worked out a plan.'

'Din' need to. I watched until there was a chance

37

and . . . here you are.'

'The ammo for that old Sharps must be so old it's dangerous to handle.'

'Still does the job.'

'Obliged, Buckskin.'

That didn't seem to require any kind of response.

Two days later, Gideon hadn't said a whole lot more but Buckskin didn't seem to mind. He and the Indian took turns in climbing up a high ridge and scanning the Moonlights.

The Indian returned from look-out duty, handed Buckskin the battered leather-and-brass field glasses.

'Posse's way over. Them hounds must be turned right around, loco, too inbred mebbe. . . .'

'Or mebbe there was some bits of Clay's clothin' scattered about that pulled 'em over that way,' Buckskin said quietly. 'Could be a couple pieces were covered with chili powder.'

The Indian's face was broad, flat, except for the prominent cheek-bones and hooked nose. His dark eyebrows lifted.

'You ever fight Indians that way?'

'Injuns taught me. Knew they were out to get Clay. Always worked on the notion that if you know a man's gonna do somethin' you ain't gonna like, even if you dunno how or when, kick him between the legs to be on the safe side. Or lay a trail that's gonna keep him a long way away.'

'Glad you on our side.'

'I'm on his side.' Buckskin nodded at Gideon who smiled thinly.

'Buck, you're as good as you ever were, thank God.

Been thinking: time I did something to help myself. Been feeling sorry for myself too long, and – well, truth to tell, I just ain't cared much what happened to me. Or my land. . . .'

'Knew you'd git mad sooner or later.'

'Not a matter of mad, just plain damn pride, I guess. I've slouched along too easy for far too long. I'm a Johnny Reb in Yankee country. I *expected* to be treated bad and I was and, partly because of Lanie, I rode with it, took more'n I'd ordinarily take without fighting back. I let it go on too long, and they almost killed me. And they're stealing my land out from under me.'

'Not yet.'

'No. But they'll find a way. And I still dunno why.'

Buckskin stood suddenly and lifted his battered old Sharps.

'No more talk. Mebbe I wasn't smart as I figured. There's riders down the slope.'

The Indian, who had climbed back up the rocks, came sliding down at that moment.

'That sheriff's too smart. Left the hounds, hired himself a tracker, 'breed named Brandy. Tracks better drunk than sober if he knows another bottle's waitin' for when he finishes the job.'

They moved fast, but even so bullets still whistled about their heads as they lashed their mounts between the trees. Bark ripped away in white strips, exploded in sticky showers, the lead ricocheting like a bunch of mad bees.

Gideon glimpsed at least six men. Abe Chance was a smart lawman, he had always known that, but he must be much better than he'd given him credit for to out-fox Old Buckskin.

They plunged down-grade and the timber, which had thickened at first, suddenly fell away so that they were exposed in large empty areas between the trees. They were young trees, too, growing after a forest fire, the foliage not thick enough to offer any kind of sanctuary.

Buckskin was leading. The Indian kept out to one side, armed with a Spencer rifle. Gideon had no idea where he had got the weapon. Buckskin had his Sharps and a big Dragoon pistol, while Gideon still had his Remington Army .44 with one spare cylinder fully loaded, and a Henry he had liberated from a Yankee during the battle of Hambone Crossing. He had a couple of boxes of rimfire ammunition for the Henry but wasn't sure how many cartridges were in each box.

Buckskin had made sure their water-bottles were full at all times and that there was jerky and hardtack in their saddle-bags. If they had to make a stand, they should give a good account of themselves. . . .

That was put to the test in less than twenty minutes.

They rode into a dead-end draw, there having been a rockfall since Buckskin had last been here, cutting off their escape.

When the posse rode in and saw the blocked draw, Abe Chance smiled. *Trapped!* he crowed silently. Then the first bullet dropped the rider beside him, sending the man rolling over his horse's rump as the animal shied away.

'Cover!' bawled Chance and the men scattered amongst the boulders, lead kicking dust and whining all round them. They leapt from their saddles, crouching among the rocks.

Only then did Chance realize that the man who had been killed was Brandy, the 'breed tracker. He felt a chill in his belly, an anticipation of much worse to come. . . .

Just who was it who was trapped here?

Then he spotted gunsmoke high on the rise of the big rockfall and Chance smiled grimly: looked like they had spooked and tried to climb clear over it, got themselves stuck. . . . Now he had them! And none of them would be going back alive!

'Shoot to kill, men! We ain't takin' no prisoners this day!' His voice echoed down the draw and reached the fugitives clearly.

Then Buckskin's Big Fifty filled the draw with thunder and two posse horses reared and thrashed, dropping as if they had had their legs chopped out from under them.

'Judas priest!' gasped one posse man. 'He got two with one bullet!'

'Shoot back, you dummy, shoot under that cloud of gunsmoke!' bawled the sheirff, his own Henry working fast.

His lead whined and spurted rock dust up on the pile but only the Sharps answered – and the posse was short of another horse.

'Git them damn broncs under cover!'

'Do it yourself, Abe!' someone snapped, even as another horse was smashed dead where it stood.

41

It was deafening in the draw now with the rolling gunfire from the buffalo-gun and the sudden volleys from Gideon and the Indian, raking the posse's shelter. There were rocks all around them, in front, to the sides, behind. The fugitives concentrated their fire into rocks behind the ridge that protected the posse. Ricochets slashed, snarled and laid brief silver streaks across the sandstone and shale. One man screamed as a flattened slug tore into his leg.

'Sheriff! Get us outta here, for Chris'sakes!'

The Sharps stopped shooting suddenly and Abe swore, feeling sick. All the horses were dead, blown to hell by those huge .50 calibre slugs. There were already crows and buzzards circling.

Then the canteen on the saddle on his dead horse seemed to explode, the carcass shuddering as the water sheeted briefly in the sunlight. The rifles up there blasted again, steadily, until every visible canteen was blown apart.

In five minutes, the posse was destroyed, one man wounded, one dead, no horses, no water. If a man was fool enough to try to retrieve his grub-sack from a downed horse . . . well, no one was that suicidal.

'I'm not through yet, Gideon, you rebel bastard!' yelled Abe Chance. 'I'll get you and whoever's with you if it takes me the rest of my life!'

CHAPTER 4

ON THE LOOSE

Gideon lay prone atop the flat rock just beneath the ledge of Wild Horse Mesa, sweeping the field glasses slowly over every part he could see of his land below.

He was pressed well back so that the overhang shielded him from the sun. That way the lenses would not flash and give him away.

Not that he had to worry: there was no one in sight down there.

His mouth tightened when the jumbled pile of charred timbers that was all that was left of his house and barns and corrals came into view. He lingered on them, changing focus as he searched this section or that. Nothing. Seemed to him the mess was just as it had been right after the fire.

It didn't appear to have been disturbed in any way.

Gideon lowered the glasses, rolled back from the edge and frowned, still looking down below. He could see all the way to Bootleg Creek, the boundary

43

between Lazy G and Bull Blanchard's Graveyard spread. He glimpsed some dust way over beyond the creek, on Bull's land. Riders working in the brush, he guessed, though he would have thought that patch of brush had been cleared of mavericks long ago. But there were other reasons for working brush than chousing mavericks, he guessed. . . .

It puzzled all hell out of him.

They had gone to a lot of trouble to put him out of the picture, hoping at first that the prospects of three months on Chance's notorious chain-gang might be enough to make him accept Blanchard's offer. When he didn't show any signs of weakening, they went to the other extreme, sent in Puddler, his mission to fake a brawl which was designed to end tragically . . . for Gideon.

Thanks to Buckskin and the Indian that hadn't worked, either. They had destroyed Abe Chance's posse – hell, the sheriff and his men might *still* be walking out of that Moonlight country for all he knew – or cared.

Now he had come down to see just what it was they were doing to his land – and he found nothing. It was lying there, untouched since the fire, which he knew now had been deliberate. Not even a man on watch or anyone from Blanchard's was showing the slightest interest in Lazy G.

Gideon had ridden in a wide circuit, studying his land from several angles, up high, to the side, down on the ground, staying well out of sight.

No one.

He simply couldn't figure it. . . .

44

*

It took him hours to make his way back to their present hideout, one they had moved to after routing the posse.

Buckskin had figured the cave was no longer safe with Chance scouring this neck of the woods and admitted he didn't have anywhere else in mind to go to immediately.

'Got just the place.'

Gideon and Bucksin had both looked sharply at the Indian. He wasn't a man who spoke just to hear the sound of his own voice.

'Lot of ridin', lot of climbin' on foot, draggin' our mounts. We can leave 'em in a canyon I know but better if we have 'em close by to where we live.'

Gideon nodded. Of course. This was Navajo country, where they had ranged in their hey-day, fiercest warriors of their time; some said the present day Apaches were an off-shoot of the early Navajos, a breakaway bunch whose sheer ferocity and wilderness skills had made them into the toughest and most ruthless fighters the south-west would ever see.

So they followed the Indian and it took a day and a half before they reached a canyon that somehow reminded Gideon of a church. Not that he was too familiar with churches, but he had been married in one. This place was like a huge circle, edged by red cliffs, and there seemed to be a strange silence that pervaded it, a *feeling* that touched deep inside a man if he was sensitive enough to recognize it as some sort of . . . communion, with . . . what? Gideon didn't know, felt awkward even thinking about it, but the sky was clear blue above, with only a scattering of small white clouds and a wheeling hawk or two. *Maybe this was once a kind of sacred place to the people who had lived here.*

Then he looked at the towering cliffs again and knew why the Indian had brought them there. These were cliff dwellings out of the Navajo's past, pueblos, long abandoned, inhabited only by the spirits of those who had once lived here. If you believed in such things.

The Indian didn't say what his feelings were on the subject one way or the other, but Gideon noticed how he walked very softly, paused briefly before entering each dwelling by the numerous interconnecting doorways carved in the rock or dried-mud walls. He also saw him quietly burning corn-husks and maize-stalks, fanning the smoke with a handful of eagle-feathers, chanting to himself in a low hum as he looked up at the vaulted sky. . . .

Gideon figured the Indian was maintaining contact with his ancestors' spirits and moved away silently. He would never mention what he had seen . . . that was strictly the Indian's own business.

But Pueblo Canyon was an ideal place to hide out. Mighty difficult to get to but once there, with near-exhausted horses, there was a clear stream and patches of grass. The dwellings made excellent look-outs: by clambering up shaky ladders to flat rooftops,they were able to see for many miles in the clear air. Only the odd rattler, coiled in a gloomy corner, or a malevolent spider hiding in one of the many pieces of ancient pottery posed any kind of threat. . . .

When Gideon found his way back after riding to check his land, Buckskin and the Indian came down from where they had been watching from one of the rooftops, both armed.

'No one following?'

The Indian shook his head. 'You move good for a white man. Buckskin says he taught you.'

Gideon nodded. 'We've known each other a long time.'

'They rebuildin' your house?' Buckskin asked. Gideon shook his head, sat down in the shade and rolled a cigarette after a drink of cool water. He looked from one man to the next.

'I don't savvy it. There's no one there. Nothing's been touched.'

Buckskin hunkered down; his leathery old face was too seamed to show whether he was frowning, but he sure seemed puzzled. The Indian's face showed nothing, except a small lift to his eyebrows.

'Figured Bull Blanchard would have a crew over there by now,' Buckskin allowed.

'No one. Men working brush over on Graveyard across the creek, but I rode all round my place and nothing's been touched. Cows are still in the pastures or they've wandered up into the edge of the Moonlights. Even the chickens that survived the fire are still pecking around the yard and the old corn-patch. Place looks like the end of the world, with all that charred timber, just . . . waiting. For what, Buck?

47

Why the hell haven't they moved in? They've got me on the run now and someone'll put up a bounty in the hope I'll be shot down. They could take over whenever they want.'

The oldster shrugged. 'Beats me all to hell.'

The Indian sat on a log. 'Why'd you buy that land?'

Gideon frowned as he looked up sharply.

'Why? Well, it was just a . . . feeling, I guess. I saw it and something clicked inside me and told me that was the place for me. When the Yankees put me to work in that St Louis Lands Office, and I found the survey map of this area, and a registry sergeant who was partial to whiskey . . .' He shrugged a little awkwardly, maybe slightly embarrassed. 'Well, I figured they were all good signs, coming together. Like I was meant to have that land.'

Buckskin's expression didn't change but the Indian nodded; he would savvy about signs and symbols and how they could affect a man's life.

'But somethin' special must've made you want that place so bad,' Buckskin said quietly, dark eyes boring into Gideon.

Clay Gideon thought about it, then nodded slowly.

'Yeah. Yeah, when I think on it, maybe there was some kinda special draw. But . . . we were in full retreat at the time, a whole heap of Yankees on our tails. . . .'

It was the end of Februrary 1865.

The South was crumbling and being swept towards the final, unconditional surrender. The starving, ill-equipped Rebs that were anywhere near their home states scattered, made their way home by whatever means they could find.

A-Troop of the Colorado Volunteers was reduced to less than a dozen survivors, but they stuck together, making for the south-west from where most of them came. They believed there wasn't a Yankee soldier within 200 miles.

Until they rode through Matchlock Canyon and into an ambush at the far end. It was merciless, the killing done by soldiers equipped with Spencer repeating rifles and with plenty of ammunition for the new butt-tube magazines. It made for continuous fire and A-Troop was reduced to four men in as many minutes – and two of those were wounded. They scattered.

Gideon had been lucky. A ball had clipped his shoulder, burned a furrow across his back, but he had managed to stay in saddle, letting himself slide down and around his horse, hanging on desperately, keeping the racing animal between him and the Yankees. A man in blue rose, sighting carefully. Gideon knew he would bring down his horse and that would be the end.

In one hand he still held his Remington pistol. He didn't even know if there was a charge left in the cylinder. But he brought it up and across the saddle, thumbed the hammer and squeezed off what turned out to be his last shot.

It must have been a fluke, but the ball took the Yankee through the middle of the face and Gideon saw the pink mist and dark pieces of shattered bone as the bullet did its work. The near-headless corpse thrashed and bucked amidst the other soldiers crowding the ridge. Men yelled in horror as they were splashed with blood and something more grisly. It threw the line into brief panic, long enough for Gideon to escape, using his swinging weight to drag the horse over the edge of a dry wash.

Earth crumbled and erupted and he fell free of the rolling animal, but skidded and half-ran down to the bottom. As the dazed, panting horse staggered to its feet, Gideon jumped from the top of a rock into the saddle, rowelled out of there, weaving through the wash and eventually emerged on the edge of a buffalo wallow. He rode down and up the far side, into a tangle of boulders on rising ground. At the top, he reined down to give the horse a blow. There were enough balls and powder and percussion caps left to reload five chambers of the Remington's cylinder. When he didn't see the Yankees he took time to charge his gun, hands shaking, spilling one packet of powder so he ended up with only four cylinders ready. It would have to be enough – and, damnit! – here they came! At least a dozen men, riding fresh horses, led by a heavy-set officer, sitting four-square, rigid with determination.

The chase lasted another two days and some Dutch settlers, old people, children, and one legless veteran in a makeshift wheelchair, helped him. They gave him a fresh horse, what food they could spare, and even a rifle. It was an odd weapon, a Dutch Snider with a folding bolt that flipped out to one side. It was single shot and there was a bag of thin cardboard tubes bound with cotton thread, charged with powder and a conical bullet in the end. One of these was dropped into the breech, the bolt flipped back, locked, and the gun was ready to fire.

'I can't take your only weapon,' Gideon told the old man.

'Take it with our blessing. Ve com here long ago and two of my sons die for the Confederacy, Hans gave his legs. All is lost now. If this vill help you . . .' He shrugged and Gideon couldn't delay any longer so he thanked them and rode away, with the dust of the Yankee patrol showing beyond the ridge behind him.

The land he rode across was green and there was a small mountain where he could see the fluid lace of a thin waterfall tumbling into a pool. Childhood pictures from an old English adventure story-book about Robin Hood flashed into his mind. A good place, this, he decided, like a glade in the Sherwood Forest in the story-book. It would be great to have a place like this – and in the back of his mind he decided he would come back here some day and file on this land if it was available – if he survived. . . .

The Snider rifle accounted for five Yankees in the pursuing patrol, killed three and wounded two. Then the weapon jammed and Gideon didn't know enough about it to work it free so he abandoned it and rode on. Eventually he found himself in St Louis, hiding out with a bunch of other Rebs on a leaky riverboat until a Yankee troop discovered them, dragged them out and told them about Lee at Appomattox. . . .

*

'Where the Dutchies were was on the edge of the land I later claimed as Lazy G, over on Bull's side.' Gideon finished his story. 'I guess if there was anything special that made me follow through on it, it was that Dutch family.'

Both Buckskin and the Indian showed puzzlement at that.

'The Yankees chasing me found the rifle, the old Snider. It was a dead giveaway. It could only have come from one place, and I had used it to kill a few of their men, wound others.' Gideon paused. 'I heard later that the patrol rode back to the Dutch place after they lost my trail – killed 'em all. The whole blame family, kids right through to the old grandparents, even the cripple. . . .'

'Not unusual,' allowed Buckskin, 'even that late in the war. . . .'

'No, I'd heard about the massacre. It was Colonel Bannister, the murdering son of a bitch. Wiping out families seemed to be his specialty . . . I went back to see if they'd been buried decent. I know, it sounds a loco thing to do, but those people saved my life and lost theirs because of it. I'd done nothing for them except bring down trouble of the worst kind on their heads. I figured I owed them something, but there was nothing I could do. They'd been buried in a mass grave; we've even turned up the odd bone after heavy rain.

The oldster said nothing, nor did the Indian. Gideon snorted, half smiling. 'Funny thing, that waterfall wasn't there when I did file on the land. Seems the Yankees had blasted down part of the mountain on top of the mass grave. To hide any trace of the murder, I guess. It changed the stream's course and it spilled down the east side of the slope, not steep enough to make a waterfall.'

Buckskin squinted at Gideon. 'You're kinda soft under that rawhide exterior, ain't you?'

Gideon shrugged. 'I've always felt bad about those Dutchies.'

'No need. Somethin' similar would've happened to 'em anyway, the kinda cut-throat gangs that traipsed that part of the country right after the war.'

'But it happened because they helped me.'

Buckskin shook his head slowly, not going to continue; he knew Gideon's way, and even took a small pride in the knowledge that he had had something to do with helping shape the man's codes.

'You think I'm nuts?'

'You are what you are, Clay.'

'Men of my tribe never forget a debt either,' said the Indian, quietly. 'A man dies, the debt is owed to his family. There is always some way to pay.'

'Not this time. Couldn't even put a cross over the grave, not with half a mountain sitting on top of them.'

'Well, it still don't tell us *why* Blanchard and his cronies want your goddamn land.'

Gideon had to admit the oldster was right.

They wanted it badly enough to kill him, yet, in the weeks he had been on the chain-gang and then on the run, they had done absolutely nothing to the land: no rebuilding, no damming of the creek, moving Graveyard cows on to Lazy G pastures. Nothing.

It surely wasn't that they were *afraid* to make any kind of a move while he still lived, with that solid land registry in his name in Washington. Gideon knew Galbally and Abe Chance would eventually find a way of overcoming that.

No, now they wanted him dead, *needed* him dead so they could move in and do whatever it was they wanted with Lazy G.

So, he aimed to stay alive no matter what, and to find out what was really behind the land grab.

And he was prepared to kill to do it.

Bull Blanchard wheeled his horse outside the gate of the ranch yard and glared at Coke who had come hurrying up. The look on the big man's face told the rancher there was trouble.

'That kid – Renny . . .'

'What about him?' Bull was in no mood to give an inch, his brittle gaze bouncing off the hardcase.

Coke didn't seem worried about his boss's mood.

'He's on the loose.'

Blanchard stiffened, frowning, taking a moment before exclaiming:

'The hell does that mean?'

'Seems he can't stand closed-in places – there's a name for it—'

'Claustrophobia. So what? Lot of people are that way. They overcome it or fight it off long enough to get their job done.'

'Kid's been in a snit for days, shakin', throwin' up, screamin' in his sleep and disturbin' the others—'

'Kick his butt for him! Christ, why d'you have to bother me with this kind of stuff?'

'He ended up sluggin' Bo.'

Bull's eyes widened. 'That kid – slugged – Bo Flynn?'

Coke managed a half-smile. 'Yeah. Bo's been havin' a bad run. What with Gideon messin' him up and his shoulder just gettin' better. Then this Renny hit him over the head with a pickaxe, on the flat, luckily, knocked him tail over tip into a mullock pile and made a run for it.'

'And he got away?' Blanchard's teeth bared as he gritted the words.

'Change of shift. Charged on through like he had the Red River flux, grabbed a hoss and lit out for the Moonlights.'

'An' you're standing here telling me about it!'

'I got men after him – Bo's leadin'.' He smiled again. 'He'll tear that kid apart if he gets his hands on him.'

'*When* he gets his hands on him! And it better be soon.'

'Renny won't get far.'

'You damn fool! He worked for Gideon! He knows the Moonlights like he knows his own name!'

'But he's in all-out panic, boss. He dunno what he's doin', just runnin', wantin' to feel space and fresh air around him. Bo'll ride him down before sundown.'

Bull's horse was skittish, impatient for its ride

which was being delayed by Coke. Blanchard fought
it irritably.

'I don't want to see that kid again. No need to
bring in the whole body. Just his ears'll do. Go tell
Bo, and *stay* out there till you get him!'

Coke didn't like that but he had no time to
complain.

Bull wheeled his mount and spurred out of the
yard.

CHAPTER 5

MANHUNT

Renny was afoot, begrimed, clothes torn from his flight through the brush. Staggering, he hit Bootleg Creek on the bend, waded out, threw himself head-long into the shallow water, ridding his eyes of the grit and dust that had collected there, fouling his sight.

Half-choking, he waded across the creek on to Lazy G land and had just pulled himself out on to the bank and was sitting there getting back his breath, when he heard a horse.

He jumped up, almost losing his balance, saw the cowboy forcing his mount through the brush and recognized Peewee, the Graveyard wrangler. They hadn't got along too well since Renny had gone to work for Bull Blanchard but he wasn't expecting the hostility that suddenly engulfed him.

Peewee hooted and whirled his lariat around his head as he rode straight at Renny. The kid, startled, surprised, jumped back into the creek. But Peewee jammed his spurs harder into the horse's flanks and the animal leapt out from the bank. Renny yelled, turning, arm going up protectively across his head as hoofs thudded towards him. He threw himself desperately aside, screamed as a shod hoof raked down his right arm, ripping shirt and flesh. But he narrowly missed being crushed under the weight of the horse. Raging now, he surged up out of the muddy water as Peewee leaned from the saddle and struck at him with the now soaking lariat. The stiffened grass rope took Renny across the shoulders and he fell, submerging.

Peewee struck again and again and Renny, gagging as he went under, grabbed the wrangler's leg, and heaved mightily, rearing up, baring his teeth with effort. Peewee gave a startled cry and was hurled out of the saddle. He clawed at the bank and Renny saw the wide eyes and immediately knew the young cowboy was afraid of being actually in the water; as with many ranch hands, it was more than likely he couldn't swim.

Renny laughed, grabbed the back of Peewee's shirt as the man tried to climb up the bank and flung him into the water. He saw the terror in the other's white face, rammed a knee into Peewee's chest and forced him under. The wrangler thrashed and choked and bawled and Renny relented and dragged him out on to the bank where he sprawled, coughing up water.

Renny, still mad, kicked him roughly.

'Why you try to ride me down, damn you?'

Peewee stared with round eyes, white showing all round the pupils.

'Bull's payin' for your . . . capture!' he sneered, edging back from the water now, feeling safer and more confident on dry land. ' 'Fraid of the dark, ain't you.'

Renny went very still.

'No – unless it's . . . Never mind what I'm afraid of! You're a son of a bitch and I'm takin' your hoss!'

'No you ain't!' Peewee reached for his dripping sixgun. Renny kicked him under the jaw, stretching him out cold.

Shaking, he grabbed the Colt, rammed it into his belt and then went to the horse which was shaking itself free of creekwater. He leapt into the saddle.

He yelled exuberantly as he lashed his mount across the flats, running for the Moonlights.

Abe Chance and his posse found Peewee sitting forlornly on the bank of the creek, nursing his swollen jaw, spitting blood. There were two broken teeth between his boots.

'He done a run,' the wrangler explained to the sheriff, words slurred, grimacing as he spoke. 'Quit Graveyard an' – stole my hoss. I figured he might try to cross Lazy G and waited—'

'The hoss your own?' interrupted the lawman.

Peewee shook his head. 'Bull's . . .'

Chance nodded grimly. 'Then that kid is now a hoss-thief – and we hang hoss-thieves on the spot.'

Peewee looked alarmed. 'I almost had him! Bull's offering fifty bucks to the man who brings him in . . .'

'Forget it, kid,' Abe Chance said. 'We'll handle this from here on in.'

He led the posse towards the Moonlights. By God, he had been made to look a fool by Gideon and his pards. No damn pimply-faced kid was going to get away from him now.

Abel Chance would show the citizens of Bannister County that he was still a hard man who knew how to do his job.

When Renny stopped to look back from Wild Horse Mesa and saw the posse coming up from the south-east, and a dust cloud in the west that had to be Blanchard's riders, his young heart flipped briefly.

Hell! Two bunches hunting him. He knew it was no good turning to Chance for help: he had seen the sheriff stagger into Graveyard with the remains of the posse he had led after Gideon had escaped the chain-gang. He saw how friendly Bull and Chance were and heard enough to know they were in this strange deal that involved Gideon's land together.

His panic had put him on the run and he sensed that they would shoot to kill once they spotted him. Peewee had said there was a bounty on his head already, thanks to Blanchard. He might be pretty dumb in general, but Renny had enough sense to realize he knew too much now and they would want to stop him passing on what he knew – especially to Gideon.

He'd been a fool to weaken and swing over to Blanchard because of the offer of more money. Now he had no money, a six-gun that wouldn't fire because the creekwater had soaked the powder charges in the cylinder, was forking a stolen horse and had no place to go.

Except that somewhere in the Moonlights he knew Old Buckskin had a secret cave to which he went occasionally. A place the old mountain man liked to retreat to once in a while when the monotony of ranch life got him down. He would never run out on Gideon, but he needed to get away to his cave once in a while, to live like he used to twenty years ago, hunting and trapping his food, making rawhide and buckskin, turning back the clock for a few weeks. . . .

Renny had tried to follow him several times but the oldster had easily out-foxed him. Except maybe one time; he had hidden his tracks, all right, and Renny had become lost trying to find his way out of the hills. He hadn't actually located Buckskin's cave, but he had smelled the smoke of the old man's camp-fire and he had taken a note of where a thin, shimmering, almost invisible thread of smoke lifted out of the boulder-shot slopes, its heat wavering as it rose skyward.

Now he would make for that place, pretty sure that it was here that Buckskin would be hiding out with Gideon after rescuing the rancher from the chain-gang.

Renny almost made it.

He didn't know he was within a frog's leap of Old Buckskin's cave when he heard a shout below. Hipping in saddle so fast he almost fell, he saw the five riders urging their mounts up the slope. A rifle barked and lead bounced off a tree beyond where he sat the weary horse before thrumming away into the afternoon heat.

Renny started his mount across the slope, heading into thicker timber, but the guns below found his range and the horse went down with a neighing sob, falling outwards towards the slope. Renny jumped but hit wrong, staggered and slid and tumbled down through a storm of gravel and dust, dead leaves and twigs.

When the dust cleared, he sat up, and felt the bile rise in his throat as Bo Flynn, his head swollen on one side, grinned down at him, then lifted his rifle and drove the butt between the kid's eyes.

It was enough to smash Renny unconscious for a few minutes and when he regained his senses he was being dragged down the slope with a rope tied around his ankles, behind Flynn's horse. The other four riders flanked him and he tried to grab the rope, take the strain, but the hard earth scraped and bruised his twisting body, turned his clothes to rags, flayed layers off his flesh.

When they stopped, Flynn dismounted and hauled the semi-conscious kid to his feet, batting him hard across the mouth.

'Shouldn'ta hit me, kid. Don't take kindly to that.'

'I – I panicked!' croaked Renny, tasting blood. 'I – I can't stand bein' closed in. . . .'

Flynn laughed. 'Well, you gonna be closed in pretty damn soon, boy – in a grave. *And* minus your ears!'

Flynn started beating Renny on the last word. The

others stood around, dead-panned, watching as the big man's fists smashed into the kid, breaking bones in his face and his ribs. When he fell, Flynn wiped the back of a thick wrist across his sweating face and started in with his boots.

'Don't forget Abe Chance said he stole one of Bull's hosses, Bo,' spoke up one of the men. 'Hangin' offence, Abe said. I ain't never seen a hangin'. . . .'

That pleased Flynn and he had the men throw a rope over a suitable branch, made a hangman's knot and slipped the noose over Renny's bloody head. The kid's legs wouldn't hold him. His eyes kept rolling upwards, exposing the whites. His trouser front darkened with the sudden spread of urine. He didn't know where he was except it was a place of unendurable agony, maybe the edge of Hell itself. . . .

Then Flynn and another Blanchard man hauled on the rope. Renny's feet left the ground and he began to convulse and kick and thrash as Flynn tied off the rope around the tree trunk. Silent, the five men stood back to watch Renny's last struggles.

Then thunder rolled down the slope and the branch that held the dying youngster shattered where it joined the tree in a burst of flying splinters. Renny crashed to the ground and lay there, still writhing as the others ducked for cover, the broken branch lying across his legs.

Other rifle shots crackled down the mountain and two of the Graveyard men staggered and bit the dust. Only one managed to drag himself behind a tree for cover. Flynn, pale-faced, gun in hand, looked wildly up the slope. But he was staring into the westering sun: the shooters had it at their backs.

The big gun thundered again and a heavy slug drove clear through the trunk of a young tree where a man crouched. He grunted and was flung back to land at the base of the tree where Flynn waited. Bo saw he was dead or dying, triggered wildly and made a run for his horse.

He almost made it.

Then something picked Flynn up and flung him, flailing and twisting, several feet, body arched like a drawn bow. He cannoned off a tree and fell, gagging, pain low down in his back, just above his right hip, where the bullet had taken him. The guns continued to blast from above, bullets biting into trees, seeking the cringing Graveyard men. Two, one already wounded, made a leap for their horses and spurred wildly away. The guns hammered. Through blurred vision, Flynn saw one reel but the man managed to hang on.

Then, while the rifles still sought to stop the fleeing men, Flynn managed to grab the stirrup of his horse. He fired his Colt, the bullet burning across the animal's rump.It whickered wildly and took off with the man dragging alongside, a hand hooked through the stirrup. . . .

During the last exchange of shots Clay Gideon had come skidding and leaping down through the trees and now he stumbled into the clearing, dropped his rifle and knelt swiftly beside the still-jerking Renny.

He had the noose loosened in a moment and

looked up as Old Buckskin arrived in a cloud of dust and gravel, holding his smoking Sharps close to his chest.

'He dead?'

Gideon pushed the blood-soaked hair back from Renny's eyes, his face grim.

'Not yet. That goddamn Flynn almost kicked him to death. Help me get him back to the cave, Buck.'

The Indian appeared then from behind the bullet-shattered tree where one of the Graveyard riders had fallen, wounded and moaning. There were no moans coming from that position now and the Navajo wiped fresh blood from his knife blade on the shirt of a dead man huddled near a log.

'That one holdin' his stirrup managed to get away,' he said as Buckskin cut Renny's bonds carefully. 'Think it was Flynn. We'll have to quit the cave now, I guess.'

Gideon agreed, told the Indian to drag the bodies out of sight and hide the horses in a draw.

It was only by chance that they were at the cave when they saw Renny captured by Flynn's bunch.

They had left the pueblo canyon, deciding that there had to be some way of finding out just what Blanchard was up to. He and Galbally and Chance had gone to a lot of trouble to remove Gideon from the Lazy G and, outwardly, at least, hadn't done anything to or with the land when they had the chance. It was mighty puzzling.

They didn't know what part of the Moonlights the sheriff and his posse were working, but they figured he would be out here somewhere, mad as a hornet trapped in a bottle, determined to track down Gideon and the Indian, not to mention Old Buckskin.

'The cave's the best place to operate from for a couple of days,' Buckskin had said. 'We can risk that long, I reckon. If we can't find out what we want to know in that time, we ain't gonna find out anythin'.'

The others agreed and made their way from the pueblo canyon back to Buckskin's cave high in the Moonlights. They had barely settled in when Flynn's bunch ran down young Renny.

Once they saw that Flynn was aiming to hang the kid they started picking off the Graveyard bunch. No mercy, but it was always hard shooting downhill, though they didn't think anyone had escaped totally unscathed. It was too bad a couple had got away, including Flynn, but they would be long gone before Blanchard was able to get any men up here to hunt the fugitives down.

It was obvious that Renny wasn't going to make it. Flynn had done too much damage with fists and boots and that brief dance at the end of a lynch rope hadn't helped. His neck was swollen and rope-burned raw and he was in much pain.

Gideon gave him water and then Buckskin pushed him aside and put his tin mug to Renny's smashed mouth. The raw red-eye in the cup stung and brought Renny back to full consciousness, or as full as he would ever make now. The kid gagged and coughed and air wheezed noisily through his damaged airways. His eyes flew open and he stared up at Gideon.

66

'You had it rough, kid.'

Renny continued to stare, blinked, then nodded. He lifted one blood-streaked hand and grabbed feebly at Gideon's shirt-front. Gideon and Buckskin both noticed the ingrained dirt under his broken fingernails. His voice was rough and husky.

'C-couldn't s-stand it, Clay. Always hated – bein' closed in. Finally – snapped, near went – loco. . . .'

Gideon pushed the blood-stiff hair-strands back from Renny's battered face again.

'It's OK, Renny. This is a big cave. I'll take you outside if you want, though. . . .'

Renny moved his head slowly, side to side.

'Don't matter – now – I'm – finished. . . .'

'You take it easy – we'll get you to a doc. . . .'

'No – time – Clay – Clay. . . .' He tried to sit up, coughed some blood, but, gasping, refused to stay quiet. 'That – graveyard – Bull was – there that day – they killed the – Dutchies. He was one of – Bannister's troop. Was him blasted – the hill top down – to cov – cover the bodies.'

He dropped back, chest heaving and Gideon gave him some more water, pushing Buckskin's hand aside with the mug of red-eye.

'You'll kill him,' he growled.

'This'll make a dead man sit up an' whoop 'n' holler.'

'Leave it, Buck. Renny. . . ?'

The kid's eyes flickered open.

'What about the Dutchies' grave, kid?'

Renny stared blankly for a while and Gideon thought he was slipping fast. Then he rallied, obviously forcing himself to hang on just a little longer.

'Bull saw – gold after the blast . . . cluster of – small – nuggets. . . .'

Gideon straightened and exchanged a startled glance with Old Bucksin.

'Gold!'

'He – covered it up, come back after the War – filed on the land. Tried for yours, too. . . .'

'Uh-huh. But that part he blasted is outside of Lazy G. The creek separates the hill from my land. If there was gold there it's all on Bull's own land.'

Renny nodded. 'He dug down. Took a long while but he – found a vein – followed it. It twisted an' turned, kept leadin' him on. He – decided to put his men on it – made us dig a tunnel – under the creek – it's almost dry, that section. Wasn't even hard but it was dark an' dank an'—'

'A tunnel! Chris'sakes, is that what you were talking about? Feeling closed in, how you got all that dirt jammed under your nails and. . . ?'

Renny was nodding, his head seeming limp now.

'I panicked – ran for it. B-Bull's got his men workin' it. The vein winds under your land, Clay. . . .'

'That's why you never saw 'em doin' anythin',' allowed Buck quietly. 'They was there all right – but underground.'

'Renny, are you saying there's gold *under my land*? That Bull Blanchard's working a damn gold-mine underneath Lazy G?'

'V-vein's gettin' – richer – leadin' to a M-M. . . .'

Renny convulsed and there were several minutes of horrible sounds and spraying blood before the young, battered body was still.

Gideon eased the dead boy back, covered his face with his hat. Still hunkered down, one hand on Renny's shoulder, he said quietly: 'I reckon I can still catch up with Bo Flynn. What was Renny trying to say just before he died, you reckon?'

'Hell, that don't take much figurin'. He was tellin' you that Blanchard's followin' that vein to the mother lode. Somewhere under Lazy G.'

CHAPTER 6

CAPTURED!

Bo Flynn hadn't made any effort to cover his tracks.

The horse dragged him for over half a mile before he let go and the animal ran on a further seventy yards before it stopped completely, turned to look at its master, then ambled over to the nearest patch of grass and began to browse.

'Lousy . . . jughead!' Flynn gritted, rolling on to his side, spitting grass and grit that had been thrown into his mouth during the drag through the brush. He had lost his hat and his shirt was torn in a dozen places, his trousers were also ragged.

But he flopped now on his good side and grunted and groaned his way to a position where he could see the bullet wound. *Hell, there was a mighty lot of blood!* He felt queasy when he saw that the leg of his trousers on that side was soaked all the way into his boot-top. He tore off his neckerchief and wadded it over the wide-open gash ripped in his flesh by one of

Buckskin's big slugs. He was lucky it hadn't chipped the hip bone or most likely he would be crippled. But he was losing plenty of blood and it scared him.

Somehow he managed to stanch the flow, partially, leastways, with the wadded neckerchief and by buttoning his vest tightly, pulling on the side-adjusting straps so that it held the wad firmly in place.

Panting and dizzy, he called to the horse but although the animal lifted its head and pricked up its ears it made no move to come to him. He swore until he was hoarse and almost sobbing in frustration. Flynn lay back, fighting for breath, eased his six-gun from its holster. A quick look showed that at least two percussion caps had fallen off the nipples. He couldn't reach the pouch that contained more as it was half-way round his belt and he gave up, just lay there, his mind wandering. He must have passed out for a time.

There were deeper shadows filling the brush with slabs of solid black when he opened his eyes, not knowing where he was, the pain of the wound setting in now and swirling through his aching body with every movement he made.

Then he heard a sound to his left and swung his head that way. His heart, already pounding like a Comanche war drum, seemed to accelerate – and then almost stop.

Clay Gideon sat his horse a few yards away, leaning on the saddle horn, his face grim as always, and a tombstone look in his eyes.

'Hope it's hurting plenty, Bo. Young Renny didn't die easy, you son of a bitch.'

Flynn started to answer, changed his mind; maybe it would be best if he didn't get smart with this tough ranny right now. 'You're scum, Bo. Never been anything else. And you're yellow, clear through to what little backbone you've got. Renny didn't deserve what you gave him.'

'Bull wanted him dead, and he's my boss.' Flynn's voice was weak now and Gideon saw the man was in a great deal of pain and needed a sawbones quickly. *Good!*

'I'll settle with Blanchard when the time comes, Bo. Tell me about the tunnel he's digging under my land.'

Flynn's breath hissed through his teeth. *Christ! The kid had lived long enough to tell him about that! Well, all that meant was that Gideon had to die – and soon.*

If Bull was willing to pay fifty dollars to have Renny stopped, what might he pay to have Gideon out of the way for keeps!

That motivated Flynn, weak and suffering though he was, to bring up his gun from the side away from Gideon, thumbing back the hammer as he did so, coughing so as to cover his movements. It cost him plenty in effort – but he was committed now, there was no turning back.

About the time he realized that his gun was missing some percussion caps, and he didn't know whether a 'live' chamber was under the hammer, Gideon's Remington blasted in two rapid shots.

Flynn's blood-stained body jarred with the impact of the balls as he was slammed over on to his wounded side. One final scream of pain was torn from him before he slumped, lifeless, a bundle of torn, bloody rags lying in the deep shadows of the brush.

Gideon looked down at him without expression, lowered the gun's hammer slowly. He wasn't a man who liked riding with only a partially loaded gun but he would have to wait a few minutes for the eight-inch hexagonal barrel and the used chambers to cool before pouring more gunpowder in and ramming the ball on top with the hinged ramrod under the barrel.

So he dropped the gun back into its holster and was sliding the Henry out of the saddle scabbard when a bullet cut air past his face. Instantly he rammed home his spurs and the horse lurched forward as he threw himself on to its neck, reins in his teeth, fighting to hold the rifle whose blade fore-sight was caught on the lip of the scabbard.

The horse was a trained cowpony and weaved expertly between trees and thickets of brush. Guns were hammering behind him and he heard men shouting.

Likely the gunfire when he had killed Bo had been heard by some of Bull's riders, or maybe even Abe Chance's posse, and they had come riding in with guns a-smoking. One of the men who escaped from up the mountain might even have reached them and started to lead them back up this way. Not that the 'why' or 'what' mattered now – he had to get the hell out of here.

At last the Henry was free and he lifted in the saddle, twisted even as he levered in a shell and raised the rifle to his shoulder. He glimpsed the riders – at least six, he thought – triggered four rapid, hammering shots. He saw bark spraying and a man's hat spinning through the air. A horse went down with a shrill whickering sound and the rider sailed over its head. He swung the rifle to the right, beaded swiftly, and fired.

But he never saw where the bullet went.

His mount let him down. Well, maybe not – it weaved and ducked and swerved, but didn't allow for its rider sitting tall in the saddle. Luckily it was a young sapling with springy branches but it still caught Gideon across the head with a force that felt like a kick from a mule with a belly-ache.

Next he knew the world was totally out of kilter, sky, trees and ground all mixed up, until he thudded down between some bushes and tried to hang on to his senses through wild arcing flashes behind his eyes. A massive jarring seemed to break every bone in his body. Then he somersaulted and bounced and skidded and once again he was alone in a dark and painful corner of some place he didn't want to be.

Abe Chance's posse had found him after he had shot Flynn, led to him by the gunfire and one of the men who had escaped from the mountain. But the man had soon become lost trying to find his way back. After he stumbled on the posse, he babbled on about the deadly fire of Old Buckskin and the Indian, still rattled by the memory. They eventually got him calmed down but he couldn't lead them back to where the ambush had happened. Only Gideon's shooting had given them direction.

Gideon's head felt like a used dum-dum when he opened his eyes and was jerked painfully and roughly to a sitting position. They flung him back against a tree and his skull hit the bark. He moaned aloud, hands going to his temples.

'Don't worry, Gideon,' Abe Chance said smugly. 'You won't be in pain for long. You're an escaped prisoner and murderer. It's my duty to save the citizens of Bannister Springs money. I can do that by stringin' you up on the spot.'

'No . . . trial?' Gideon croaked, spitting some blood. 'The judge won't like that. Missin' out on all that publicity.'

The sheriff scowled, hesitated before answering:

'You leave the judge to me!'

'Glad to. But it won't look good, will it? Lynching me, when everyone knows you and Galbally and Blanchard want me outta the way permanent. Someone might figure it was mighty convenient. . . .'

'Be too late then. 'Specially for you!'

Some of the posse laughed and the sheriff ordered a man to bring a rope. They prepared it, deliberately slowly, where Gideon had a good view of the making of a hangman's knot. It gave him a queer feeling; he had seen exactly the same thing only a few hours ago when Flynn had been going to lynch young Renny.

'Renny told me about the tunnel, Abe.'

Chance looked at him slowly, eyebrows arched. 'So?'

'Buckskin and the Indian were with me when he did.'

Chance's face straightened.

'They were marked to die anyway. This'll just hurry things along a little.'

'You've got to find 'em first.'

'We'll find 'em.'

'Or they'll find you. Wonder how many of you'll get back to Bannister Springs alive?'

The man making the noose stopped, snapped his head up, glanced, with some alarm at other posse men who knew just how deadly Buckskin and the Navajo were. The ambush survivor's shaky telling of the details was fresh in their minds. Their wide eyes searched the deep shadows of the brush. One man jumped when a twig snapped – or maybe only a small dead branch fell of its own accord from one of the trees.

'What was that?' the man croaked and they all dropped hands to their gun butts; it had been a long manhunt and they were edgy, eager to get back to their families in town. Now Gideon had planted a new fear in them.

Gideon, despite his pain and bruising, smiled with bloodstained teeth.

'Pick off the sheriff first, Buck!' he called suddenly, startling everyone, and Chance lunged at him, punching him in the face, clapping a hand over the bloody mouth. But Gideon bit him and Abe snatched his hand away. 'Take your time, Buck! Make it a good shot. In the gut where it'll hurt like hell!'

The lawman snarled and gunwhipped Gideon unconscious. Breathing hard, he looked around at the rest of the posse, saw – and maybe felt – their fear.

76

'He's bluffin'! There's no one out there!'

'That's what you said just before they bush-whacked us and shot up our canteens and killed our broncs! Judas, Abe, those two are deadly! Look what that stinkin' old mountain man done to the chain-gang guards!'

'You see 'em? Huh? *You see 'em?*'

'Goddamnit, I don't have to see 'em! I dunno as I've ever really *seen* 'em – only what they done, pickin' us off whenever they pleased! Settin' us afoot without water!'

'Goddamnit, there's no one out there, I tell you!'

But the uncertainty was well and truly undermin-ing the posse now and the sheriff knew it. Truth to tell, Abe Chance wasn't too keen to stay out here in the Moonlights with night barely an hour away and the thought of that Indian and the old mountain man on the loose, stalking them.

Making up his mind, he turned to the brush-choked slope. 'You make a move agin us, first one to die'll be Gideon!' he called. 'I mean it! You kill one of my men, Gideon's dead two seconds later! You hear?'

No answer, of course.

'All right. Here's what's gonna happen. We're takin' Gideon back to town, gonna lock him away, give him a trial if we have to.'

By that, he meant if Judge Galbally forced him to go to trial, make things 'official'. The old judge was a greedy, ruthless man, but he was very conscious of his position, had been appointed by the Reconstruction Committee itself. There was a promise of some mighty fine prospects if he did his job well. And right now the Reconstruction needed to have a good image. Other countries were beginning to baulk at offering their help to rebuild America.

Mostly because the Yankee victors were still strutting and showing their deep hatred for the Rebs. But it had gone on long enough. It was time to move on, do some *real* Reconstruction, get the country back on its feet. To do this, the Yankees needed to have better co-operation from the interested overseas countries, but mostly from the conquered South which had been battered and kept down on its knees for far too long. Right now the North needed the South.

Galbally had tried to explain this to Chance and Bull Blanchard, but both men had seen it only as the judge's ambition getting in their way: they wanted no delays in their plans. This gold-vein promised vast riches for them all, so it was no longer enough to have Gideon 'sell' Bull his spread, even if they could forge the papers well enough to pass muster. The only real answer was to have Gideon *dead*, then all arguments would be superfluous about ownership of the land called Lazy G . . . and the gold that was on it.

Galbally might willingly order Gideon's execution for his crimes, but he would want it done so that *if* there ever was an investigation it would show up on the books as having been according to law: trial, judgment and sentencing.

Abe, impatient and looking for revenge on Gideon after what he saw as personal humiliation when the posse had been reduced to slogging all those miles back to civilization without even a sip of water, had been going to jump the gun by ordering Gideon's hanging on the spot, because his hatred for the Reb was all-consuming.

But now he had calmed down some. It was Gideon himself who had made him see that Galbally would insist on a trial, with all the outward appearance of being perfectly above board, but with only one end for Gideon; the gallows.

By using the potential threat of Buckskin and the Indian he didn't even have to back down in front of the posse; all he had to do was make it look as if he was agreeing with them, that they *were* in danger, and they had talked him around, and he was offering them safe passage by using Clay Gideon as a hostage.

'Come on, let's get down outta these hills and back to town. They ain't gonna shoot us, long as we got a gun to Gideon's head, I guarantee it.'

Buckskin and the Indian were out there, all right.

They had been about to start picking off the posse men when Sheriff Abe Chance had called out his threat to kill Gideon the moment one of the posse was shot.

The Indian, crouched across the rock ledge from Buckskin, saw the oldster lower the huge side hammer on the Sharps and take the rifle out of the forked rest he had been using to support the barrel for a steadier shot.

'Son of a bitch! That puts a spike in things.'

'We take the sheriff first, then the others will scatter. I don't think they are very brave.'

79

'Me neither. But Abe's give 'em the idea now. We can nail him but someone'll shoot Gideon just the same.'

The Indian nodded. They would all die, of course, if they did but Gideon would be dead, too, and that made no sense.

'They got us, Buckskin.'

The oldster nodded slowly, watching the posse make its way down the darkening slopes.

'Maybe more'n you know. They take Clay into town to jail, they'll expect us to bust him loose. They'll have the whole damn town waitin' for us.'

The Navajo's look was sharp and grim.

'There must be a way.'

'Sure. But can we find it before they stretch Clay's neck?'

CHAPTER 7

PRISONER

Gideon was surprised to find a letter delivered to his cell with his supper. It was from Lanie.

He glanced up coldly, watching Chance through the bars.

'It's already open.'

'Yep.' A challenging look but no attempt at explanation.

Gideon was even more surprised when he read that Lanie was missing him: *and, believe it or not, my dear husband, I am even missing the ranch, despite all my complaints...*'

She had returned to her people who were holidaying in Denver, and admitted now that it was a letter from her mother urging her to go and join them that had decided her to leave the ranch. Now, she wasn't at all sure that she had made the right decision. Her parents would be in Denver for a few more weeks and she had decided to stay with them, holidaying, but giving deep thought to her future: *our future, Clay. I do love you and I know now I acted like a spoilt child in many ways. I don't wish you to get your hopes up too much but I will write again and tell you what I decide. If I do come back, I hope you will welcome me. . . .*

Gideon could hardly believe what he was reading: it was a complete turn-around. Was it possible Lanie had come to her senses? Hell, was that the right thing to say? Or even think? True, they had parted on a reasonably friendly note but she had made it sound pretty damn final.

This is not my kind of life, Clay – I'm sorry. I just can't endure this style of living any longer. . . .

And she had boarded the stage fighting tears, hadn't even glanced in his direction as the Concord pulled out of town.

The other thing was: did he want her to come back? Especially now: no ranch, himself a wanted fugitive, on track for a short trip to the gallows. There was no point in her returning to this mess.

They had set his trial for three weeks ahead, an obvious ploy to allow them that time to keep working on the underground vein and searching for the mother lode which Blanchard seemed certain sure was on Gideon's land.

'The hell with it,' he said aloud and then called for Abe Chance, a deputy, anyone.

The sheriff himself came, cold and remote and suspicious as usual.

'I need writing stuff. Have to write a letter to my wife.'

Abe shook his head.

'No letters allowed out.'

'Dammit, Abe, I can't provide for her and I have to make her see that or she'll be hounding me till you drop that trap-door under me on the gallows.'

Chance's grin widened.

'I do like to see you with a slew of problems, Gideon! 'Specially those you ain't able to do anythin' about. Ain't got nothin' agin your wife, but it's her own fault for marryin' a Johnny Reb like you.'

'Do I get pen and paper or not?'

Abe merely laughed, turned and started down the passage, picking his teeth.

'Told you the rules.'

'Come on, Sheriff! You know I don't have that much time! I've got to let her know. . . .'

Several hours later Pete Dane the amiable turnkey came on duty. He was a friendly type and Gideon had always gotten along pretty well with him. He put it to Pete to bring him writing-materials. Pete frowned worriedly.

'Sheriff'd have my hide, Clay. Sorry.'

'I've got a good hunting-knife among my things in the front office. You know the one. You've often admired it. It's yours, Pete. I need that pen and paper, *amigo*.'

Pete Dane did a lot of hunting and Gideon's knife *was* a good one, a small Bowie blade with a special curved tip for skinning animals with tough hides. Pete thought about it, went away, eventually came back with the writing materials.

Of course it was well past 'lights-out' but Gideon managed to write what he wanted in the dark, chasing a shaft of moonlight as it angled through the bars.

When Pete was going off-duty the next morning, Clay asked the man if he would mail the letter; he knew if Chance or his hardcase deputies got wind of it, they would likely rip it open and read it or simply screw it up and toss it away. And Pete Dane would be in a lot of trouble. But he also worked part-time in the general store which had the postal concession, each morning. He could slip it into the mail bag easily.

'Costs money to mail a letter,' Pete said slowly, sucking at a hollow tooth and grimacing as the cold air hit the decay. He rubbed at his jaw. 'Got me some dental work comin' up, Clay.'

Gideon took off his left boot and peeled back the leather inside. He had a silver dollar there and offered it to the man.

'It's all I've got, Pete. Buy yourself a drink with what's left over after the postage.'

Pete slowly brightened, reached for the money and the envelope – in that order – and promised to see it went out in the morning's mail. Gideon hoped he would keep his word. Likely he would – he was an easy-going type.

Clay had told Lanie in his letter how things stood here at present, said the land was hers if Blanchard and his cronies didn't manage to steal it away from him. But his future looked too bleak for him to even contemplate the possibility of her return. He didn't exactly tell her he would welcome her back, but he did allow that he missed her and wished she hadn't left when she did, although in one way he was glad, because he wouldn't want her here right now with so many enemies closing in on him.

He felt he had had to tell her the situation and advised her to see a lawyer and maybe get some kind of hold put on the land which would ensure that it at least passed on to her. It would be worth a few thousand dollars, he reckoned, and he had tallied 700 cattle only two days before she left. A smart lawyer ought to be able to do something for her. . . .

Abe kept armed guards around the jail night and day. He wasn't taking any chances of Gideon escaping, with or without help.

The time passed for Gideon like treacle leaking from a can in mid-winter. He was allowed to exercise in an adobe-walled square twice a week and could wash daily, but the rest of the time he was kept in the cell, an armed guard in the passage.

He heard nothing of Blanchard's progress on the gold-mine, which was how he thought about the tunnel the big rancher was working now. Chance wouldn't even talk about it. The sheriff's only conversation with his prisoner was to taunt him about how tightly the judge had the charges sewn up and how the newly built gallows was attracting a lot of attention in town.

'Stand on your bunk and pull youself up to the barred window and you'll see the top of it,' the sheriff told him. 'Bright new pine, rich in resin and smellin' mighty fine. Likely be the last thing you smell before the stink of brimstone in hell, Gideon, 'less you count the cloth we'll slip over your head!'

The lawman sauntered away down the passage, chuckling.

Gideon stretched out on the bunk. There was nothing he could do. *God almighty, but it was frustrating!* Buckskin and the Indian couldn't help him the way Chance had him guarded and the place sewn up tight. He hoped they wouldn't try. No sense in them getting caught or killed as well.

Then, one week before the trial date, he heard loud voices in the front office, a definite argument, and shortly afterwards the door to the cell-block opened and a small group, hard to make out in the dim light, came down the passage towards his cell.

He sat up slowly, felt as if his jaw was hanging open like a swinging door. Chance was there, his face like a summer thunderstorm, with a well-dressed man, youngish but with a look that said he had been around. And there was a woman beside him who only came to his shoulder, very straight, very businesslike.

His heart leapt, thinking at first it was Lanie. But it was a stranger, a dark-haired, green-eyed woman about thirty who gave him a flashing smile and offered her small gloved hand through the bars.

'A pleasure to meet you at long last, Mr Gideon. I'm Roberta McHugh. I'm an attorney at law from the Denver firm of Cassidy, McArdle and McHugh. Your wife has hired me to defend you in the coming trial. Shall we make a start right away? I believe there is not a great deal of time.'

'How the hell did he get word out that he was in trouble?' The voice boomed angrily across the gloomy, dark-wood-panelled chambers and Judge Galbally glared and winced at the same time, grabbing his stomach as he watched Abe Chance shrug at his question. Then the judge burped and looked somewhat relieved.

'Don't see that it matters much now. She's tearin' all over the County, with that feller she came with. And people are talkin' to her. She could charm a grizzly, so I'm goin' out to see Bull soon as I leave here. Don't want her pokin' her nose into that mine—'

'Goddamnit! You should've gone there first!' The judge, a man not noted for his mobility or quickness of movement, suddenly stood behind his desk, face congested. 'Get out there right away, Abe! Make Bull close down the workings if he has to, but keep that damn lawyer and her sidekick out of it!'

Abe set his hat on, figuring now he wasn't going to be offered a glass of Galbally's fine imported French brandy, and made for the door.

'You know her, Judge?'

Galbally hesitated.

'Know of her and her firm. Highly regarded in legal circles. The "McHugh" is her father, ready for retirement, has a fine record and they say this "Bobbie" McHugh, as she calls herself, is more of a firebrand than he ever was. Always standing up for "people's rights" for God's sake! She can make a lot of trouble for us, Abe. You head it off or we're all through.'

It wasn't like Galbally to admit his worries openly like this, so Chance took him seriously and wasted no time in getting out to the Graveyard spread.

Bull Blanchard stepped out on to the porch and called to him to come on up to the house for some refreshment.

When they were settled with drinks in the rancher's office, Abe gave Bull the news and saw the way the man's heavy shoulders tensed, the narrowing of those bleak eyes, the whitening of the knuckles that held the glass of whiskey.

'How in hell did that happen? Last thing we need is some bony-fidy lawyer pokin' his nose in here. *Her* nose, for Chris'sakes! Abe, we're makin' good progress with that tunnel under the creek, the vein's widening, getting thicker, man! Couple of weeks, maybe less, and I reckon we'll hit the mother lode, and there's every indication it could be a *reef*, big as a goddamned house!'

Chance choked and coughed as some drink went down the wrong way. His brows arched at the rancher.

'How . . . big?'

Bull Blanchard gestured easily.

'*Big*! And it's well and truly on Gideon's land, no way anyone could say different. All we gotta do is dig it out . . . after we get rid of Gideon.'

'Then you better hold off makin' the breakthrough till after we hang him. Once he's dead, it won't matter.'

Blanchard's cold eyes bored into the sheriff and he frowned, squirming a little.

'How d'you know?'

'Wha—? Hell, the judge said if he's dead, then

there's no one owns the land so we're home and free. . . .'

Bull continued to stare as Abe's words gradually trailed off. Suddenly the sheriff straightened in his chair and he sucked in a sharp breath.

'Aw, Jesus! His wife!'

Blanchard nodded gently.

'You said her letter to him was tryin' to patch things up. If he leaves her the land . . .'

The sheriff thought about it.

'Ah, the judge'll take care of that. He'll know what to do so she can't touch it.'

'Thought you said he was leery of this legal bitch?'

'Well, yeah, he did sound a mite . . . worried.'

'It's somethin' none of us thought about. And it could stop us dead.'

Abe tossed down the rest of his drink now, obviously worried.

'I'd better see if the judge realizes just what . . .'

Bull stood abruptly, lifting a big hand.

'Forget the judge. He's a nervous-Nellie right now, not wantin' to upset the Administration so's his own retirement'll go along smoothly. He'll want to keep this gold under his hat till he's a long ways from here. It'll be a mighty big bonus for him.'

'For all of us. But why don't you want to remind Galbally about Gideon's wife? Likely he'll think of it himself and—'

'And what?' demanded the rancher. 'What'll he do? That damn "Bobbie" comes from some big law firm in Denver which does a lot of work for the Administration. She's throwin' her weight around, and he knows she's got a reputation for always shoutin' about people's rights and so on. It'll have his ulcer spittin' like a volcano and he won't know whether he's on his head or his tail. The judge knows her father, likely respects him. He'll realize she's nothin' but trouble, all right, and can turn all our work upside down, but by then it could be too late for all of us. No, we've got to take care of this ourselves, Abe.'

Chance started to back off. It showed in his half-crouched body and the way he stood to the rear of the chair he had been sitting in, watching Bull closely.

'I hope you ain't thinkin' what I think you're thinkin', Bull. . . .'

'What're you lookin' so worried for? Hell, it's a cinch; she'll want to inspect the tunnel, see how far we've dug under Gideon's land—'

'Well, that'll sure be the end of everything, once she realizes that the main gold-lode ain't on your spread!'

The rancher smiled crookedly and poured two more stiff drinks, handing a glass to the sheriff. He lifted his own glass as if in a toast. Voice sounding bleak and determined, he said:

'To the memory of the hot-shot Denver lawyer, Miss Roberta McHugh. Killed doin' her duty in a tragic accident in a mine-tunnel collapse. Down the hatch, Abe, ol' pard, down the hatch! We got work to do!'

CHAPTER 8

COUNSELLOR
McHUGH

Gideon was more interested in news about Lanie than the interrogation that Roberta (call me Bobbie} McHugh put him through.

'Look, Clay,' the woman said with a touch of exasperation. 'I've tried to reassure you several times that your wife is fine, staying with her parents in a good Denver hotel, concerned only for your safety. Lanie is a friend of mine and I want to do all I can to help. That means helping you. But I need your co-operation.'

The quiet young man who had accompanied Bobbie McHugh was standing at the door of the cell, arms folded. She said he was called Hush because he never talked much and when he did it was in a voice that was little more than a whisper.

'He's my assistant, does research and most of the

running around for me,' she had explained when she first entered Gideon's cell.

Sheriff Abe Chance had wanted to stay but she gave him a withering look and reminded him that any conversations between an attorney and client were strictly confidential and that if the sheriff did not allow them privacy she was sure that even Judge Galbally would provide the necessary legal order to obtain this.

Sullenly, Chance had left and gone to see the judge.

'I'm glad you didn't tell Lanie in your letter that you might be hanged, Clay,' she went on. 'At the same time, if you had notified her earlier I could have done a lot more than I'll be able to now.'

'I thought she'd left for good and had no more interest in me.'

Bobbie McHugh smiled slowly. 'If you could only see her! A bundle of nerves and anxiety. She wanted to come with me but her parents insisted she stay. I'm glad they did because I can work better without having to concern myself with Lanie's anguish as well.'

That was good news to Gideon, though he wished, too, that she had come. He had a feeling that he might never see her again. Bobbie was honest enough to tell him that she feared the judge would tie things up, legally, so she would not be able to do much before Gallows Day, as Chance called it happily.

'But I can tell the judge is concerned that things look right. He wants to impress the Administration

92

Council and I think he has ambitions for a place on it.' She shuffled her papers and notes. 'The escape from the chain-gang, I think I can get reduced to that and no more. Men died, yes, but you had nothing to do with that. It was your rescuers—'

'I don't want Old Buckskin in any more trouble than he's in already. The Indian, neither.'

She shook her head slowly.

'Buckskin killed those guards on the chain-gang. But I can't concern myself with his troubles right now, Clay, you're the one in custody, in the shadow of the gallows, so you must have priority. The ambush of the posse gives me a great deal more trouble. You were with Buckskin and the Navajo then; killing legally sworn deputies is a very serious matter, and I believe there can be no good and sustainable excuse for it.'

Gideon sighed. 'All right. I dunno as I killed any of them but there's no way I can prove it.'

'But you did shoot Bo Flynn in cold blood.'

'He tried to shoot me. I didn't know his gun would misfire.'

'No-oo. But once again, he was a duly sworn deputy.' She stopped suddenly, frowned. 'Or was he? Did Bull Blanchard merely send along a handful of men to help out, or did Sheriff Chance take the time to swear them in as deputies?' She made rapid notes. 'This is something I need to check right away.'

She stood and Hush opened the door far enough for her to squeeze through. Outside the bars she turned to speak to Gideon.

'I think I'll be able to get a stay of execution,

temporarily, but it's time I need to look into a few things. And I'll certainly investigate your allegations that Blanchard found gold on his land and followed the vein through on to your land. . . .'

Gideon stood and crossed hurriedly to the bars. He looked from the girl to Hush.

'You be mighty careful of Bull. He's arrogant and ruthless. If he smells real gold . . .'

Bobbie smiled. 'Clay, I'm an attorney, a junior partner in a nationally respected law firm. I think even your Bull Blanchard would think twice about harming me.'

She started off bouncily, enthusiastically, and Gideon frowned. He caught Hush's eye.

'You watch out for her. A Denver lawyer won't mean a thing to Blanchard if he figures she's gonna make trouble for him.'

The slim man nodded slightly, turned and followed his boss down the passage. Gideon went slowly back to his bunk and started to build a cigarette.

He wouldn't let his hopes get too high, but there was something about that woman lawyer that made him feel a little better about his future.

Or what was left of it.

The Indian came in silently as always and didn't see Buckskin at first. Then there was a faint movement in the shadows of the canted boulder near the entrance to their shelter. Dim light touched worn blue metal in Buckskin's gnarled hands and the Indian heard the big hammer lower quietly.

They had a small hideout amongst some rocks high on the west side of Wild Horse Mesa. Only an Indian would know of such a place and, while it was draughty and not fully sheltered from rain, it was an easily defendable hideaway, from which they could watch both Graveyard and Lazy G, as well as the trail to town.

'You been gone long enough. What you find out?' Buckskin asked and the Indian could tell from his enunciation that the oldster was wearing his stag-bone teeth. *That peccary he killed for supper last night must've been tougher than he thought.*

'There's a girl – a lawyer. She's workin' for Clay.'

'Well, there's a puzzle! But how in hell did you get close enough to find that out?'

'Know the swamper at the Razzle Dazzle. Chance's still got all them armed guards on the cells. No way to get to Clay.'

'There has to be! Judas, they're gonna hang him in a few days!'

The Indian nodded, squatting, taking a piece of cold meat from a flat rock near their small fire. He tore and chawed and wrenched before he had a piece he could work between his strong teeth. *Tough all right. . . .*

'We need a fire.'

Buckskin stirred. 'The hell for? There's enough meat there to see us through till tomorrer. An' we don't need to show any more smoke than we have to.' He stopped and frowned when he saw the way the Navajo was looking at him.

'A . . . fire! You mean . . . in town?'

95

The Indian nodded.

'Keep 'em busy while we get Clay out.'

Buckskin shook his head.

'Chance'll never fall for it. He'll double the guards, let the townsmen fight the fire.'

'Bank is only clapboard.'

'Yeah. But there's a brick room inside where they keep the money.'

'General store – saloon – livery. No townsmen'll let them burn.'

Buckskin sighed. 'Mebbe not. But how you gonna set all them fires? We can't show our faces anywhere near town. There's bounties on us and them Yankees'll put a slug in us at first sight.'

'Know how now.'

Suddenly Buckskin smiled, the worn bone teeth showing dull grey against his brown skin.

'You sounded just like a Reservation buck then! Say, how come you speak such good American, anyway?'

The Indian took his time answering.

'I'm the last of my tribe, Buckskin. They tagged me Navajo but really it's Havasupai – nearer Hopi or Zuni. Buried my mother, the last of my family, two years ago. Sickness took my people; I was lost. Knew no one. No one spoke my language. I had no one. A band of hunters found me and took me back to a town. They locked me up and some professor came to see me, wanted to study me, to know about my tribe and their ways because my people had been a breakaway tribe of the Anasazi. I had to learn American.'

96

Buckskin waited and the Indian shrugged.

'They fed me, clothed me, gave me medicine. I told and showed them all I knew. That professor died and the others weren't interested, only in putting me in a medicine show – a freak. So I walked out one day and came back to my old country.'

'Well, we sure ain't noted for our good treatment of Injuns in general, I give you that. You got a name?'

The Indian glanced at him sharply.

'My name is with me and the Great Spirit only. I will hear when he calls.'

Buckskin seemed a mite uncomfortable at such talk.

'Yeah, OK. But how come you took up with Clay on the chain-gang? And how come you were even there?'

'I like the old ways of hunting. I made a bow and arrow and shot a white man's cow for meat. It belonged to Bull Blanchard.'

Buckskin grinned. 'I'd've helped you eat it. But Clay? You never stuck to any other white man in that gang.'

'They leave me alone in there. But Clay tried to talk to me, in Apache, which I savvy a little, and Comanche. He didn't know I spoke *anything* but he tried to communicate, kept on trying. So I thought maybe here was a white man worth knowing.'

'Yeah, well, he is. He saved my neck long ago. That's why I cain't just set still and watch 'em hang him.'

The Indian stood slowly. He had been carrying the roll of buckskin that he used for his rifle and the old

97

mountain man was surprised when he unrolled it and removed the rifle, followed by an unstrung bow and cedar-shafted arrows with flint heads – seventeen in all, the good medicine number – in a mountain lion skin quiver, fur side out.

'Judas! No wonder you were gone for so long. What'd you make that for? Gettin' low on ammo?'

The Indian stood and placed one end of the bow against the arch of his left foot, bent the sinew-backed mulberry wood into an arc, and slipped the loop of the deer-tendon string over the top, settling it into grooves. He plucked it and the bow thrummed. He almost smiled as he turned to Buckskin.

'Had this stashed away. Knew I'd use it again one day. Now it'll save Clay from the gallows.'

Judge Galbally was furious, and trying hard not to show it.

'How dare you come in here with your big-town ways and tell me what you're going to do! I'm the Judge Administrator of this County and you ask my permission for every damn thing if I say so!'

Bobbie McHugh sat at her ease in the judge's chambers, Hush standing as still and quiet as a statue by a window, arms folded. Bobbie smiled at Galbally.

'And I'm sure you will say so, Judge. You're aggravating your ulcer over nothing. I simply asked if the posse was duly sworn in before Sheriff Chance led the men out to pursue Gideon and his friends.'

'Did you ask Abe Chance?' the judge hedged.

'Of course. He, too, got angry and refused to

answer, told me to come and see you.'

'Quite right. You're trying to upset our routine, Miss McHugh, and I'm here to tell you that I will not stand for it. I run this County as I see fit – er – according to rules and regulations, that is, and I will not have someone from—'

'You already told me, Judge,' Bobbie cut in and watched the man's face take on a deep purple hue. 'It's a simple question and requires the simplest of answers: yes or no. If you are unable to tell me then I must assume that in the hurry to recapture Gideon the deputizing of the posse was overlooked. If so, I believe I can make an excellent case for the dropping of murder charges against Clay Gideon.'

'Deputized or not, those men were killed by Gideon and his friends!'

'Yes, but he had a right to protect himself and if he was shot at by a bunch of men, ordinary townsmen forcibly recruited by the sheriff, he had every right to shoot back. I think I will make my application for a stay of execution along those lines, Judge.' She stood abruptly and Galbally started a little. 'I'll get a wire off right away. The Governor of the Territory is a good friend of the family so I don't think he'll mind if it arrives around his supper-time – or even later.'

Galbally was practically blowing steam jets from his flared nostrils. His big old hands crumpled papers on his desk.

'I'm warning you, miss! No one threatens me in my own chambers!'

Bobbie was a picture of innocence.

'Threaten?' She glanced at Hush. 'I heard no

threats, merely a casual statement of fact. You know, you sound a little paranoid to me, Judge – if you'll forgive me for saying so—'

'Get out! And take your dummy with you! Send your damn wire or whatever. But until I get personal instructions to the contrary from the Governor himself, Clay Gideon is still set down to hang on Friday. . . .'

Bobbie smiled as Hush opened the door for her.

'We'll see, Judge. Thank you for your time.'

When she had gone, Galbally went to his liquor cabinet and hurriedly uncapped a decanter of his imported brandy.

He spilled most of it before he got the glass half-full, then tossed it down, took a deep breath, and refilled the glass. He gulped a mouthful, steadied himself and sat down again, holding the glass in both hands as he sipped slowly.

That was better. He was calming down gradually, but his stomach still felt all churned up. This damned woman attorney – *They should never have allowed females to study law; he had been saying so for years!* – was going to be a pain in the butt.

And she was letting him know it.

The Governor was a friend of the family!

That was enough to shake anyone up. It was time this blasted female met with an accident.

At once he got the stabbing pain in his stomach and just under his ribs where his ulcer was giving him pure hell.

He dispensed with the glass this time and drank straight from the bottle.

*

Outside her hotel, Bobbie turned to Hush.

'I don't think we'll trust the telegraph office here, Hush. The judge and Chance wield too big a stick. Would you mind making a fast ride to Durango to send off my message to the Governor?'

Hush frowned. 'I'll do whatever you want, Miss Roberta,' he whispered. 'But I can't get back before tomorrow afternoon. Will you wait till then before going to see this Blanchard?'

'I don't think I can waste that much time, Hush. I'll be all right.'

'I think Gideon meant it when he said Blanchard was a very dangerous man. Please wait till I get back.'

She saw his concern was genuine, as always, and placed a hand lightly on his arm.

'I'll go see the families of the men who rode with Chance in that posse and see if they can tell me for certain whether they were deputized.'

Hush knew it was the best he could hope for and sighed.

'You have a gun of some sort?'

She patted her embroidered handbag and smiled.

'In its special pocket in my bag.' The pocket was actually camouflaged under a flap which, unless studied closely, appeared to be merely part of the bag's front. But a tug on the ribbon-rose adornment would release a clip and it could be swept aside, revealing the flat little pearl-handled derringer with its twin loads of .41 calibre bullets in a special let-in pocket. 'I do have another – but that's special, as you know.'

Hush didn't look any easier.

'I don't think you'll be able to get Gideon's charges reduced to self-defence.'

Bobbie nodded soberly. 'Perhaps not. But it's only a delaying tactic. The more time we have, the better chance Gideon has of surviving. Even if he faces a long jail term. That's better than hanging, surely.'

Hush said nothing, but he thought that Clay Gideon hadn't seemed like a man who would be happy spending years in jail. He looked to Hush like a man who would prefer to take his chances, even if it meant being an outlaw.

Anyway you looked at it, this was a mighty explosive situation.

CHAPTER 9

FIREFLIES

Roberta had more success than she expected, questioning the families of men who had ridden in the posse Abe Chance had gotten together to pursue Gideon and his pards.

The men in the original posse, the ones who had had their water-bottles shot to pieces and their mounts killed, setting everyone afoot, had been duly sworn in as deputies, except for the half-breed tracker who had been killed. But after they had eventually gotten back to town, not a single one of them wanted to get fresh mounts and supplies and continue the pursuit. They wanted only to stay with their families.

Raging, Abe Chance had stormed into the Razzle Dazzle saloon, picked half a dozen men at random and *ordered* them to arm themselves and join his new posse. Those who demurred were threatened and they reluctantly followed the sheriff out of town into the hills, picking up some extra men at Blanchard's Graveyard, who joined only because Bull ordered them to. Those folk who had lost husbands or brothers in the shoot-out at the mesa had been told by an angry Chance that there would be no pay or compensation as they were not legally deputized and his office was short of funds.

So, with a bitterness that even overrode the fact that the men were killed by the fugitives, the kinfolk gave Roberta definite proof that the only man in the second posse backed by law was the sheriff himself.

It might still be hard to claim self-defence as Gideon *was* a fugitive, but it would certainly bring down the murder charge to something less. And if she could get some kind of proof that the presence of gold on Lazy G land was behind Gideon's persecution, she was sure she could save him from the gallows. Anyway, her father would bring his years of expertise to bear and help her if she asked him to.

Excited, *too* excited to wait for Hush's return, Roberta McHugh hired a buckboard from the livery and drove out of town at a fast rate.

Hush had hired two horses so that when one tired he could switch mounts.

He wanted to get to Durango with Miss Roberta's message to the Governor as fast as he could. He knew how enthusiastic she could be, how she could get carried away with the case she was working on, throwing caution to the winds. He recalled three occasions in the last two years where he had had to go in with guns blazing so as to save her neck.

By the time he approached Apache Pass, it was late afternoon and the high walls threw cool black slabs of shadow across the trail through the break in the sierras.

An old hand at sensing danger, Hush slowed his mount, the other animal coming up alongside, not expecting a break in pace right now. But Hush kept moving, approaching the pass slowly, his gaze searching the rims of both high walls. They were in shadow; it was difficult to make out any detail.

Then he thought he saw something: a movement of black against blackness. A fleeting impression, perhaps someone changing a cramped position, or even an animal moving across the broken face of the wall.

It was enough.

Hush rode on. He had been through this pass before, with Apaches after his scalp. He recalled how the approach he was making angled to the left inside, putting any rider against a slab of light-coloured sandstone, thereby making him a good target for anyone waiting in ambush.

It was a move he had utilized himself, picking off four of the five Apaches and ending it by fighting the survivor hand-to-hand. He still had a jagged knife-scar across his belly; he had made it out alive but he had never forgotten how close he had come to dying.

So his mind recalled every detail of the approach to the pass: the entrance trail veered left to that sandstone slab, but to the right. . . ? Nothing. Only a pile of boulders from some long-ago rockfall. He smiled thinly.

He stood on the saddle of his mount, clutching his rifle, and clambered up into the fall of boulders. Then he flung his hat down into the face of the startled spare horse. It reared and swerved in fright, ran on into the pass, veering left because there was no other way to go. By then, Hush was settled amongst the rocks, a shell levered into the rifle's breech, in time to see movement up there in the high darkness as the dry-gulcher rose for his shot, keyed-up, hearing the drumming of the spare mount's hoofs, expecting a ride. The gun whiplashed three times as soon as the horse's head appeared against the sandstone slab, the echoes smashing back through the canyon, at least one bullet ricocheting. The horse squealed and then Hush fired, levered, fired again.

The man above swayed, staggered, started to turn towards him. But he was hit hard and he slipped and fell, bouncing and thudding down the slope all the way to the bottom of the pass.

Hush waited, letting the echoes die away, then he climbed down, mounted and rode in, rifle butt on his thigh. The spare mount was dying and he knew he would have to finish it with a bullet. But first he had to check and see who the dead bushwhacker was.

He was kneeling beside the man when the gun roared from above, higher than the first man's position, and he knew even as the lead slammed him on to his back that there had been a second killer, waiting, making sure he didn't escape the first trap. Hush triggered awkwardly, jerking instead of squeezing, and the gun jumped from his hand. He realized then that he had been hit in the shoulder of his gun arm.

The pain had not yet started but the arm was numbed. He rolled as another shot kicked gravel into his face, grunted as he fell on his wound, kicked off a rock and twisted on to his other side.

His pistol was in his hand now and he saw the man up there clambering down to get closer for the killing shot. Hush picked him off with two fast shots and the man floundered. Hush's gun misfired – likely a percussion cap had come loose while he was rolling around – and the wounded killer lifted his rifle, firing just before he toppled forward and down.

Hush slammed over sideways, twisting to sprawl face down in the dust.

'You've only made the damn girl more suspicious than ever!' snapped Judge Galbally as he and Chance watched Roberta drive out of town in the hired buckboard.

Abe Chance let the curtain fall back across the window in Galbally's office.

'Well what the hell was I to do?' he said. 'She went to the kinfolk of the posse. I couldn't head her off. And they're all bitchin' about their men not bein' paid.'

'Another stupid move on your part! This is no time to be playing the piker! Anyway, she must be suspicious already! That's why she never sent that telegraph to the Governor through our office!'

'Yeah, well don't worry about that. I sent a couple men on ahead to fix that dummy she runs with. They'll get him in Apache Pass before dark. Likely lyin' there dead right now.'

'I hope you're right. Because if you have another look at the dust she's raising with that buckboard, you'll see she's taken the fork to Blanchard's!'

The sheriff shifted the curtain again hurriedly and swore.

'Bull's right, Judge. She has to be stopped!'

He was surprised to see that Galbally was sweating, dabbing at his face with a silk handkerchief.

'Yes. It's – it's the only way, I suppose. But I don't like it. Her father's too important. He's an adviser to the Governor as well as the Administration Council. There'll be hell to pay over this, Abe, you mark my words. She can only be – eliminated, if there's no other way.'

'Which way?' Chance gritted sardonically.

But he was thinking about the judge's words and the man's naked fear. Galbally was right. If her messenger was bushwhacked in Apache Pass and then the girl herself met with an 'accident' it would look mighty damn strange. Suspicious. . . .

'God knows who the Governor'll send in to investigate, if anything happens to her,' Galbally moaned, wiping his hands now.

Chance looked at him steadily.

'How about – how about if Gideon was dead?'

Galbally looked at him sharply.

'Well, that's been the whole purpose of this exercise, but to make it look like he died all legal and by due process. But this woman's gathering evidence that may not only stay his hanging, but even get him off completely. And, of course there's his wife. . . .'

'We could miss out on all that gold!'

That made the judge straighten up; an equal share in that promised gold was a major part of his plans. But he had to decide just how much of a risk he wanted to take. . . .

The sheriff suddenly started for the door with long strides.

'Judge, you find yourself somethin' to do tonight. Get yourself invited out to dinner or somewhere a lot of good respectable folk'll see you. I got me a feelin' there's gonna be all kindsa hell raised in this here town tonight – could even get so out of hand that it might end in a lynch party. . . .'

Pete Dane stared at the sheriff uncomprehendingly. They were in the law office, the lawman just reaching down his hat from a wall peg, speaking over his shoulder to Pete.

'No need for you to come in tonight, Pete. Meant to send word but I been busy.'

Yeah, busy talkin' to every damn roughneck in town, Pete Dane thought. He had been stacking barrels behind the Razzle Dazzle when he had seen the lawman going from one man to the other, sometimes speaking to tight little groups of some of the worst troublemakers in town. Pete figured he had been giving them a warning – as he often did – about cutting up rough, but no one had seemed hardnosed about it. Later, poking around like the stickybeak he was, he had learned that the barkeep had been instructed to serve drinks to the men the sheriff had spoken to, and to put it on Abe Chance's bill. (Which, of course, would never be paid – if

109

O'Bannion, the saloon-owner, was foolish enough to ask for his money, he knew he would be out of business overnight, so he went along with the fiction of the sheriff's 'bar account'.)

'You'll need someone to watch Gideon, won't you, Abe?'

'Do it myself. Got me a toothache that I know damn well is gonna keep me awake all night. I gotta watch my fundin', Pete. Be just for tonight. I'll try an' give you extra duty to make up for it.'

Pete was not a bright man, but he figured it all sounded kind of fishy to him. The sheriff was holding the street door for him now, looking impatient.

'Come on, Pete!'

'Er – I left my best pipe under my stool in the passage last night, Abe. Only be a minute.'

'Well, lock this door after you. I can't stand around all night waitin' for you.'

'Yeah, you go get some medicine in the Razzle for your tooth, Abe. I'll lock up.'

Chance, distracted by the swirl of thoughts spinning in his brain, nodded and hurried off. Pete went into the passage and down to Gideon's cell.

'Howdy, Pete. Set for another night?' Gideon was stretched out on his bunk but started to sit up now. 'How about a few hands of friendly poker through the bars? I'm gonna die of boredom before they get a chance to string me up.

'Ain't comin' on duty tonight, Clay.' Pete didn't even check for his pipe because he knew it was safe at home on his parlour table. 'Sheriff says he's gonna do it hisself.'

Gideon came to the bars, frowning. 'Not like Abe.'

Pete told him about the sheriff's 'toothache' and how he had seen Abe talking with many of the town's roughnecks. 'Charley Hannah and his bunch and the Ringo brothers who've got their cousins in from the hills. I mean, them two clans are ready to fight at the drop of a hat any time, but when they're likkered up.' Pete shook his head and whistled. 'I ain't gonna be there when they square off. But I'll have plenty of extra work come mornin', I reckon, fixin' up the saloon, swampin' out the mess they make.'

'Why would Abe buy that trash drinks? He's had 'em locked up in these cells more times than I've had hot suppers.'

Pete shrugged. 'Dunno, but it sounds queer. Just thought I'd tell you.'

'Why?'

'Well, you always treated me right an' if they do act up and Abe arrests 'em, he's gonna throw 'em in here. Some're bound to end up sharin' your cell. They could git mighty rough. They're all Yankees, you know.'

Gideon felt a tingle run through him. His hands involuntarily tightened around the bars.

'Listen, Pete, do me a favour. See if you can find that lady lawyer, Roberta, and tell her I might need her help tonight. Why're you shaking your head?'

'I was cleanin' out the stables when she come in an' hired a buckboard, said she had to go outta town.'

'She say where?'

'Nope. She was lucky she could hire anythin' with wheels.'

111

'Why's that?'

Pete shrugged. 'For some reason Bull's kept his crew out on the spread, won't give 'em leave to come into town. So he hired the other buckboards to send out a bunch a whores from Sadie's Sin Bin with a load of rotgut from the Razzle to keep the boys happy.'

Likely doesn't want 'em talking about the gold, Gideon thought, then groaned.

'Damn fool woman! She's riding high, figures she's got Bull and the judge and Abe just about beat. Surely she ain't loco enough to go see Blanchard alone! Hell! And it's already dark!'

'Yeah. An' listen to that! They're startin' up in the saloon!' Pete's eyes widened.

Gideon heard the shouting from the saloon down the block, the sounds of shattering glass and splintering furniture – and then a couple of gunshots.

'Well, it's too late to do anything now, Pete. In twenty minutes I'm gonna have this cell full of fighting Yankees, likkered to the eyebrows and . . .'

Pete's face had lost colour and he started away quickly down the passage.

'I gotta go, Clay! Sorry. I – gotta – go!'

Gideon rattled the bars and shouted after Dane to give him a chance, let him out, but he heard the man run out of the front office and slam the door after him. He swore.

Not a brave man, Pete Dane, not brave at all.

And where the hell did that leave him?

Sheriff Chance triggered his Colt a fourth time,

shooting up into the bar-room ceiling, and this time it looked as though the brawling men were going to take notice.

Tables and chairs were splintered. The recently repaired bar mirror was reduced to only a few jagged shards again and O'Bannion was wringing his hands, cursing the drunken hardcases.

'All *right*!' bellowed Chance, glaring at the men he had incited to this riot, acting it up for the other saloon patrons. 'I warned you men if you started trouble it'd be the chain-gang for the lot of you. I see I'm gonna have a full cell block but I gotta show you, when I lay down the law I damn well mean it. Now line up an' start marchin' down to the jailhouse!'

The battered men looked at each other, blood trickling, skin scraped and hanging, bruises and swellings beginning to show.

Charley Hannah, a big, bearded man in work-stained clothes, sniffed and wiped blood from his bulbous nose. Link Ringo, the leader of the much-feared Ringo clan from the Moonlight back hills, glared back at Charley.

'The hell you lookin' at!'

'Dunno. The label musta fell off.'

That brought a guffaw from the Hannah faction and some of the spectators crowded back against the wall. But the Ringos weren't amused and they closed in on Charley and his backers, fists already flying. No one even heard Chance's fifth shot and the sheriff swore.

Damnit, this wasn't how it was supposed to be! These hardcases had agreed to stage a brawl and let him lock them

*up – temporarily – in the cells where they would turn on
Gideon and – well, anything could happen when such men
were all fired up with the Razzle's rotgut. . . .*

Abe Chance figured that such a bunch turning on
a lone Johnny Reb trapped in the cell with them and
causing his death would look better than a lynch
mob. He could claim that he had done his duty as a
lawman, but had been powerless to stop the killing in
his over-crowded cells. . . .

'Hell with you, Chance!' spat Charley Hannah and
he moved in on the lawman with two of his offsiders
as they dodged blows from the Ringo mob.

Chance triggered again, but the click of the
hammer falling in a misfire was lost in the racket of
the brawl. The sheriff turned to run for the batwings,
but the Ringos got to him first. Chance fought hard
and wildly but was on the losing end right from the
start. No one wanted to be locked up, temporarily or
otherwise. They knocked him down and boots swung
into his body. Someone straddled his chest, grabbed
his ears and rapped his head up and down in five
crashing blows against the floorboards.

He slumped unconscious.

'Let's lynch that goddamn Reb— He's only eatin'
grub we gotta pay for,' yelled someone. 'Let's string
the son of a bitch high enough to spit on the moon!'

That met with roaring approval and some of the
spectators joined in the shouting, jostling bunch that
crammed through the batwings and spilled out into
the dark. Two men yelled that they had ropes at the
ready as they charged along towards the jailhouse.
Then one of Hannah's group stopped, blinking,

pointing up to the sky.

'Hey! Will you lookit that! Fireflies!'

That unexpected word slowed the lynch mob and they all looked skyward.

Sure enough, it seemed that there were six or seven large fireflies streaking across the stars, one after the other, reaching apogee, before hesitating briefly and then arcing down towards the town.

'Never seen fireflies as big as that!' slurred Charley Hannah and was mighty suprised when Link Ringo agreed with him.

But Pete Dale, watching from a shadowed store-porch knew they weren't giant fireflies.

They were fire arrows – and they were falling on to the town's wooden buildings.

CHAPTER 10

NIGHT PEOPLE

Pete started yelling 'Fire! Fire!' but no one took any notice of him, the crowd surging on down the street towards the jailhouse.

They were almost at the door when he called hoarsely:

'Lookit the damn general store, you blamed fools! *Look*!'

Charley Hannah frowned. One hand tried the handle of the law office door. He registered that it was locked, then turned to ask who the hell was talkin' about the goddamned general store now, when they – *Judas Priest!*

'The store's afire!' he yelled, stunned as he saw flames leaping up behind the falsefront, shingles already burning and popping.

'I been tryin' to tell you! Half the town's burnin'! They weren't fireflies for Chris'sake, they were fire *arrows*!'

116

The mob heard Pete this time and men were shouting:

'The livery's burnin', too!'

'Oh, my God! My shop's goin' up in smoke!' That was the barber who had tagged along to see the fun. Now he was running frantically towards his small shop, shouting for someone to help him beat out the flames.

'Hell! There goes the court house. . . !'

It was true; the old clapboard building with its timber half-dome above the entrance where there was a paint-peeling depiction of Blind Justice holding the scales was enveloped in flames, the weathered timber with the tarpaper covering burning with an intensity that lit up half of Main.

'Git pails!' someone yelled, looking round wildly. 'Some blankets, too, we can wet down . . .'

'What about that old hand-pump from the blacksmith's? We can drop one end in the crick and pump water on the fire,' a shaky voice suggested. 'Three men on each side bar ought to do it.'

It was a good idea but when put into practice the mud clogged the intake and Sam Weatherby, the blacksmith, allowed he could piss faster than the stream of water that trickled from the nozzle. Back to the bucket brigade. . . .

The lynch mob was now fighting the fire's spread like everyone else; it was instinctive for anyone who lived in a mostly timber-built town. Fire was the greatest fear, always at the back of every adult property-owner's mind.

Flames were roaring, taking on weird shapes as

they blew about wildly in the twisting winds they themselves generated. People were shouting and running about, glass was shattering. Men were trying to save what they could from inside the general store; some were 'saving' items for themselves, and horses were squealing and running wild down the streets and alleyways as they were released from the inferno that the stables had become.

Pandemonium reigned and no one seemed to have any interest in the jailhouse now. Charley Hannah's group and the Ringos were fighting the fires with great effort, though a couple from each clan sneaked back to the saloon for a few drinks on the house. Until O'Bannion appeared with his scattergun and cut loose with a couple of shots that splintered more of his furniture, but cleared the barroom. Except for Sheriff Abe Chance, still lying unconscious, on the floor. O'Bannion settled down on a stool behind his bar, scattergun now reloaded. *No free drinks tonight, boys!*

He swore he wouldn't leave until the fire came in through the goddamned batwings and singed the bar front.

Clay Gideon heard all the commotion and could see the glow in the sky over Bannister Springs, occasionally the tip of a writhing set of flames. He knew that it was a big fire and suddenly realized he was locked up here in the jailhouse by himself. No one to hear any cries for help!

He stepped up on his bunk, jumped so he could grab the bars of the high window and pulled himself up. Heat touched his face instantly and he squinted, saw the livery was not much more than a skeleton framework now, beams engulfed in flames beginning to burn through and collapse. Beyond he could see the general store going up like a giant firework, the court-house dome, too. *Judas Priest!*

He started to yell but dropped back to the bunk when a voice from behind startled him.

'C'mon. Let's get outta here, Clay!'

Old Buckskin was working on the cell door, trying to find the right key on the big ring he held. He must have grabbed it from the wall peg behind Chance's desk in the front office.

'You set the town on fire?' he asked, holding the bars tightly as Buckskin worked with another key.

'The Indian. Used fire arrows. Ah!'

The door swung open. Clay grabbed his hat and lurched out into the passage. Smoke was coming into the jailhouse now and rasped his nostrils. They went to the front office and grabbed Gideon's guns from a cupboard whose door the rancher kicked in. He would have liked some spare powder and ball, too, but the other cupboards were locked and Buckskin kept telling him to hurry up and get the hell *out!*

They did, using the side door which Buckskin had forced earlier. The oldster pointed down the alley.

'I want to go out to Blanchard's, Buck.'

Buckskin skidded to a halt, shocked at the suggestion. Clay stopped, too, turning to the oldster.

'I believe Roberta's out there. She thinks she's got Blanchard over a barrel with Abe and the judge. If he

119

gets a notion she's gonna nail his hide to the wall and stop him getting to that gold, he'll kill her.'

'Well, now, ain't that interestin'!'

Both men wheeled as Gideon recognized the silhouette of Pete Dane standing in the alley mouth, backlighted by the fiery glow on Main. He held his cocked rifle.

'Judge Galbally just offered a thousand bucks to whoever catches the son of a bitch who set these fires. I ain't as dumb as you think, Clay. I figured the fire was a decoy so's someone could bust you outta jail – and sounds to me like I might git a whole lot more'n a thousand bucks outta this if I play my cards right, eh? Whaddya say?'

Then he fired suddenly as Buckskin brought up the heavy Sharps and the mountain man reeled, not firing the big gun. Gideon drew his Remington, not even sure if the gun was loaded, and thumbed the hammer. It blasted Pete Dane back out of the alley so that he cannoned into the wall and went down on his knees, slowly doubling over, as his rifle fell.

Gideon grabbed Buckskin's arm and dragged him down the alley.

'Bad?'

'Just burned my ribs. Dammit, he's tore up my buckskin shirt, too, the bastard!'

'Let's *go*, Buck! Where're the horses?'

The Indian was waiting for them on the rock ledge where he had built his fire in a hole surrounded by stones to hide the glow. He still had five or six arrows left, the shafts wound for six inches above the points with pitch-and-turpentine-soaked rags.

'Might use 'em later,' he said, gathering his gear. 'On Blanchard's ranch if we get a chance.'

Gideon settled into the saddle of a dappled grey horse: he didn't bother asking where the animal had come from. When the Indian learned they *were* heading for the Graveyard spread, he held the reins of his skittish mount, turning it towards Gideon.

'We really gonna take on all of that bunch, Clay?'

'Have to check it out. Roberta came all this way to help me.'

He let it hang. They knew what he meant and moments later they were racing along the trail to Blanchard's ranch.

'Didn't see Chance back in town but it won't take him long to find out you've gone, Clay,' Buckskin said, riding alongside and holding a bloody cloth against his wound. 'That Pete'll likely tell him anyway. You shoulda finished him off.'

'Pete's not too bad, Buck, but none too smart, either. I reckon he'll give us a chance to get away before he says anything – *if* he does. He'll want to keep in Abe's good books so he'll say something. Just don't know how soon.'

'Well, way I see it, it's mighty risky goin' to Bull's. He musta heard that part. Chance'll bring his posse there for sure.'

'I owe that woman, Buck.'

There was finality in Gideon's voice and the mountain man decided to leave it; there was no arguing with Gideon when he took that tone.

But when they reached a grassy bench that allowed

them to see the Graveyard spread, they reined down in surprise.

Lanterns were burning on strung ropes above benches and plank tables. They could see plenty of food and many bottles as well as a couple of beer kegs. There was a fiddle and a harmonica sending plaintive and off-key notes winging towards them across the darkness, men and women dancing.

'Hell! A goddamn wingding!' breathed Buckskin. 'Must be someone's birthday. Hey! I think it could be mine!'

Gideon grinned. 'Sorry, Buck. Pete told me Bull's trying to keep his men on the ranch: so they don't let slip about the gold in town, is my guess. He sent for a couple of wagonloads of whores and lots of booze.'

'They'll be busy for quite some time, I guess,' said the Indian quietly. 'If we don't see this lawyer woman, we could go check out the tunnel, see just what Blanchard's been doin' – how far under your land he's workin'.'

That sounded like a good idea and they ground-hitched the horses out of sight in a thicket of juniper and huckleberry, took their rifles and started on foot towards the lighted area. There, someone was now singing – a woman, hoarse and out of tune but getting plenty of cheers, mainly because she was only wearing a black corset and stockings that stopped half-way up her thighs, revealing an expanse of soft marble-white flesh.

The three men stretched out in long grass across the small creek Blanchard used for his house's water supply. Sounds from further along to their left told

them a man and a woman weren't interested in dancing or listening to the singing, or anything else
much, except each other right now.

They waited silently and shortly two figures stepped
across the narrowest part of the stream, adjusting
clothing as they hurried to rejoin the main group.

Gideon stiffened and the Indian, lying close
beside him, felt the movement.

'See her?' he asked. 'All I see is whores crawling all
over them cowboys. Not that I'd recognize her,
anyway.'

Gideon waited a few moments before he answered.

'Yeah, I see her.' Another hesitation, then he
added: 'She's the painted whore with the black hair
piled on top of her head, sitting in Coke's lap down
by the big beer keg.'

Several of the ranch hands had all wanted to 'try out'
the new whore when she arrived, but big Coke had
shouldered his way through and taken over.

He frightened Roberta with his proprietorial
manner, the way he bullied the other sweaty, half-
drunk cowhands, and held her arm as he led her
around, tried to ply her with booze. So far she had
been able to refuse except for when he had slipped
up to the ranch house and brought back a small
silver flask containing some of Bull Blanchard's
French brandy.

Actually, she was glad of the little extra Dutch
courage it gave her; she would need more than that
to see her through the night that was coming up, she
thought.

She was still somewhat surprised at herself for what she had done – and accomplished!

It was a spur-of-the-moment thing. She had taken a wrong turning and it was already dark by the time she found the road again.Rounding a bend in the trail she had had to rein down swiftly to avoid a buckboard slewed across, blocking the way. Lanterns were swinging in the hands of the half-dozen whores as they struggled to fit back a wheel that had come off after hitting a deep pothole. They told her that the driver, a man from the whorehouse named Hadley, had been drunk before they even left town and was now snoring in the back of the canted vehicle while they struggled to set things right.

Ginger Tallis, a large carrot-topped lady of the night with top-heavy bosom, looked Roberta up and down and told her they had been hired for a party Bull Blanchard was throwing for his crew. The 'ladies' were to drink it up and do whatever it took to keep the men happy at all times – for as long as the men wanted or could stand the pace.

'He must think a lot of his cowboys,' Roberta remarked, looking thoughtful, and, hopefully, ignorant of what kind of man Blanchard really was.

'Dunno about that, lady, but it's costin' him plenty.' Ginger leered a little and punched Roberta lightly on the shoulder. 'Ain't so hard on us gals, acshully. The boys get a little red-eye under their belts and think they can go all night long.' She guffawed loudly. 'Don't they wish! But we been paid for all night, anyway. . . .' She paused and looked Roberta up and down. 'Now, if you was to join us, we'd have an even easier night. The boys'd be queuin' up to get to you: new blood's always popular. Why, even big Bull himself'd come runnin' if he knew you was available.'

Roberta smiled but declined, watched while the women struggled to re-set the wheel with much sweat and effort, but in the end had to leave it; replacing it was beyond even their combined strength, in addition to which they didn't really know what they were doing.

'Damn that no-good Hadley! Just listen to him snore! We'll never wake the son of a bitch!' Ginger paused as Roberta reached out to touch her arm.

'Ginger, maybe you could all travel with me in my buckboard. There's plenty of room. . . .'

Ginger worked her painted eyebrows up and down.

'Change your mind, honey?' she asked slyly, joking.

'I – just might have.' The reply stunned Ginger and before she could answer, Roberta said quickly: 'I'd like to surprise Bull. He doesn't know me, but we have mutual acquaintances. One of them actually said to me before I left Denver that if I got a chance to play a practical joke on Blanchard, something that would make him look really foolish, he'd be so grateful he would consider offering me a full partnership in the law firm I work for.'

It was a lie, of course, and it sounded outrageous to her, but she had had a notion of how to get close to Blanchard instead of simply arriving and identifying herself as an attorney who was going to frustrate his plans to become rich at Clay Gideon's expense. That really would be getting off on the wrong foot and who knew what kind of a reaction he'd give to that, a man like Blanchard?

She was already regretting her high spirits which had set her on this trail to the Graveyard ranch in the first place.

She explained quickly to Ginger who was smiling broadly before she had even finished.

'I like it, honey. I *love* it. We'd all like to get back at the Bull. He ain't exactly tender with us gals and we always earn our money when he visits – which ain't often, I'm glad to say. But if you think you can handle it and you're game enough. . . ?'

Roberta McHugh swallowed, feeling her heart pound.

'I – I'm game. And I'd be glad to have your help in – any way at all . . . I could even donate a little – financial something to your evening if you'll allow me.'

There was no question about *that*, and the ladies, all smiles and twittering now, contributed some gaudy and skimpy clothing from the hold-alls they had brought along, plus plenty of cosmetic paint.

As the driver snored on drunkenly in the back of the tilted buckboard, Roberta was transformed from a nice-looking and demure legal lady into an over-painted but still attractive whore, with her hair piled up on top of her head, the carefully arranged clothing showing some interesting cleavage and a length of white leg to mid-thigh. There were plenty of tips on how to behave and keep a man interested.

Roberta's face flushed a deeper red than the rouge on her lips.

'Heavens! I won't be going *that* far! At least, I hope not. . . .'

Before they continued on their way they tipped the drunken driver out of the original buckboard into a gully with a trickle of muddy water in the bottom. He didn't even stir, just continued to snore as he flopped on his side in the slush.

They pushed the buckboard into the same gully with the fallen wheel and turned the team loose.

Then, with Ginger at the reins, they continued on their way to Bull Blanchard's ranch, singing raucously:

'Buff'lo gals're comin' out tonight, comin' out tonight, comin' out tonight –
Buff'lo gals're comin' out tonight, gonna dance by the light of the moon.'

'Gonna do *somethin'* by the light of the moon, anyway,' called Missouri Molly in her coarse voice. 'But I wouldn't bet on how much dancin' gets done!'

Roberta was somewhat startled to find heself laughing along with the others.

CHAPTER 11

WILD NIGHT AT GRAVEYARD

At first, Gideon didn't know what to make of Bobbie's transformation into one of the visiting whores.

'Has to've done it so's she can get close to Bull,' Buckskin allowed and the Indian agreed. Clay nodded slowly.

'I guess that's it, but – well, fellers, she sure didn't strike me as having enough guts to make a move like that. But there was *something* there just the same, a kind of toughness, something that set her apart from other lawyers, and not just because she's a woman.'

'Well, she's sure showin' *that* part!' Buckskin allowed appreciatively, squinting hard as he watched Bobbie McHugh fence with Coke, pushing his hands away. 'Hell, that Coke must be boss of the Wanderin' Hand Society! Hey! You see that? She just slapped his face.'

Gideon was watching, found himself tensing up. He knew Coke, knew the man wouldn't take a slap from man or woman, had seen him knock down a Mexican girl one time in the street when she slapped him for taking liberties with her. No one had intervened, not with a man like Coke when he was reeling with a load of redeye steaming him up. He had made the girl crawl away on hands and knees, pistol shooting close to her, making her scream in terror. Lanie had pulled Gideon away when he had started forward.

Now he was surprised to see Coke stand up abruptly, holding Bobbie by the shoulders so she didn't fall, looking down bleakly into her tense face. He shook her and some of the noise faded as others watched.

But then Coke grinned tightly, said something that made Bobbie quickly try to spin away. Coke caught her wrist, pulled her roughly against him, suddenly clouted her on the jaw with his fist. He must have pulled the blow, otherwise her jaw would have been broken, Gideon thought.

As Bobbie collapsed, Coke ducked and lifted her effortlessly over one shoulder, her arms dangling limply down his back. He turned and strode out of the lighted area towards the big ranch house.

'Hell! He's takin' her to his bed!' growled Buckskin.

'He sleeps in the bunkhouse with the rest of the crew,' Gideon said tautly, aware of the way his hand ached where he gripped his rifle. 'He's taking her up to Bull!'

They all knew how roughly Bull Blanchard treated women and the Indian began to fit an arrow to his bow. When Gideon looked at him quickly, he said:

'Silent.'

Gideon reached out and stayed his movements.

'You might hit the girl.'

He could just make out the indignant look the Indian threw him. But the Indian lowered the bow without drawing it.

Gideon was already moving silently, crouching as he stepped over the narrow stream at one of its bends. He followed it behind the bunkhouse. The party sounds were going full blast again and covered any noise he might have made as he flattened himself against the wall, waited for Coke to appear as he passed the bunkhouse on his way to the main building.

He moved with the swiftness of a striking snake and just as silently. He heard Coke's gasp of surprise but it changed instantly to one of pain as Gideon's rifle barrel smashed across his midriff. The big man's legs began to fold and Gideon stepped in, dragged the semi-conscious girl from Coke's shoulder and planted a boot against the sagging man's chest. He thrust him away roughly, holding the girl with one arm, and heard Coke writhing in the dust. For good measure, Gideon kicked him in the side of the head and Coke went limp.

Gideon threw the girl over his left shoulder, retreated the way he had come. The Indian and Buckskin met him at the creek bend as he waded across this time, not wanting to jump while holding

Bobbie so precariously. She was starting to come round, moaning a little.

'We gotta get outta here, unless you killed Coke.'

'Just knocked him out for a while.'

'Like a fire arrow on Blanchard's porch?' the Indian asked with a note of eagerness Gideon had never heard before. 'Or one of the barns? The bunkhouse, maybe?'

Gideon was about to say no, but abruptly changed his mind.

'Can you do it without being seen?'

'No. But that won't matter. There's no one over there who's more than ten per cent sober.'

'Bull's still up at the house, stone-cold sober,' Gideon reminded him.

'We'll be long gone before he gets around to lookin' for us,' Buckskin said, obviously eager for the Indian to lob his fire arrows on the Graveyard buildings. 'Let him take his shot, Clay. . . .'

'Right!' Gideon made the snap decision, already moving with the girl starting to struggle a little. 'See you back at the horses.'

The Indian didn't bother lighting a small fire: there was no need. He still had the pitch-and-turpentine rags tied on the arrows, wrapped around with bits of rawhide to stop evaporation as well as stickiness. Buckskin knelt and struck the vestas as they crouched behind some brush and the Indian sent the first blazing arrow arcing towards the hay barn. It *whooshed!* and the sound brought a few heads up over there at the party. Several jaws hung slackly open as the fiery arrow plunged through the open door of the barn and into a stack of baled hay. Fire was almost instantaneous, as were the sudden startled yells from inside as a woman and two men, clutching disarrayed clothing, came charging out, wide-eyed.

While they held the attention of the others, the Indian loosed three more arrows, two into the stables, one into the bunkhouse shingles. He had two left and while someone yelled and pointed in the general direction of where the arsonists crouched, no one took any notice.

The blazing buildings were sobering the men fast, setting the whores running.

The Indian's next arrow thudded into the butt end of a whiskey keg, knocking out the wooden tap, and in seconds there was an explosion of pale blue and yellow fire blossoming like some exotic giant flower, spreading like water from a fountain.

As the party area blazed, the last arrow slammed into the front porch of the ranch house, showering sparks and globules of blazing pitch on to the weathered boards and wicker seats and tables.

They heard Bull Blanchard's frantic voice bellowing at the men battling the fires in the other buildings:

'Let 'em burn, you damn fools! Save the house! Christ almighty! Are you deaf? Save the goddamn house!'

'Party's a mite hotter than they expected,' said Buckskin as they spurred away into the night. He sounded mighty pleased, he had been waiting to really get back at Blanchard ever since Gideon's ranch had burned, and this seemed to be the night for it. 'Bull'll rip this country apart looking for us.'

They slammed into a bend in the trail and saw Gideon ahead, the girl draped across his saddle and starting to struggle hard now.

'Where to, Clay?' the Indian asked, raising his voice a little.

'Where Bull won't think of looking for us. Just follow me.'

Behind them the night was lit up by the flames of the burning ranch, the roar of the fires drowning out the frantic yells and curses of the men trying to extinguish them.

'Who was it? *Who the hell was it?*'

Bull Blanchard, clothes blackened and holed from hot ash and sparks, wiped a hand across his dirty face and blinked sweat from his eyes.

His near-exhausted men, some sobered-up, some still feeling the effects of the booze and the whores – who had, incidentally, taken Roberta's buckboard and set out for town – stood around, hangdog, clothes ragged and filthy, as smoke still curled up from some of the burned buildings.

One of the barns had been completely destroyed, the one where all the hay for winter feed had been stored; the other was more singed than sustaining any real damage. The stables were a mess on one end, uprights having burned through and the broken roof sagging clear to the ground. All the horses had been saved and some men were helping the wrangler get them into the corrals, although a few had run off into the night.

The bunkhouse wasn't badly damaged but the front of the ranch house had suffered, part of Bull's office wall was eaten completely through, the big carved front door he had imported from Oregon was no more than a slab of charred timber now. Some windows had shattered, of course, and the porch roof would have to be totally rebuilt.

Angry though he was, Blanchard knew he had been lucky. He could easily have lost the whole blamed kit and caboodle.

'Well? Who was it did this?' he roared again at his shabby, exhausted crew.

'That damn woman had somethin' to do with it, I'll bet,' Coke said. His head was lopsided and he rubbed at his painful midriff, cringing inwardly at the savage look Bull threw him.

'*Which goddamn woman*? There were eight or ten here. You mean one of the whores did this?'

Coke shook his head, very carefully; his brain felt loose and he was still nauseous. 'Dunno who she was; *said* she was new – name of Cindy. I'd never seen her before an' she was a looker but I'm here to tell you, she was damn hard to get down to business. I was beginnin' to wonder about her when she kept stallin', seemed interested in seein' the big house. Asked would I show it to her.'

Bull frowned, glaring around at the others.

'Any one know what the hell he's talkin' about?'

Some of the men murmured helpfully.

'She came in with Ginger an' the others.'

'Had a few years on her but she was better lookin' than them usual dogs we get.'

134

'She was damn choosy! Wouldn' let me near her!'

'She looked kinda . . . I dunno, like she wasn't sure what to do or somethin'.'

'What?' growled Coke. 'With her looks? It sure weren't her first time, I can tell you that.'

'How you know? You never got nowhere. She slapped your face before you could—'

The man broke off as Bull stepped forward, looking hard at Coke.

'You let a whore *slap* you?'

'I din' *let* her, she done it and I gave her a right hook on the jaw, knocked her silly. Was bringin' her up to the house for you to have some fun with when—'

'When what?' Bull snapped as Coke hesitated.

'Someone jumped me. When I come round the whole ranch seemed to be on fire and . . . she was gone.'

'Back to town with the other whores?'

'No. She wasn't here when we was fightin' the fire,' one man said. 'I looked for her. She wasn't here, boss. She'd gone by then.'

'It was fire arrows done it,' spoke up another cowpoke. 'I seen 'em droppin' in—'

'Christ! Now we got goddamn Injuns!' Bull scrubbed at his singed hair furiously. 'Seems to me we gotta find this damn whore, whoever she is. She musta had somethin' to do with it. Coke, take some men and git after Ginger and the others. Drag 'em back here and we'll get to the bottom of this – or there'll be some graves to dig!'

*

They hid out on Gideon's land.

It was near the creek, but the entrance to the dry wash was choked with brush; a horseman could ride on by only yards away and never know there was a small gulch beyond that thicket.

The girl had been semi-conscious for most of the ride down from Blanchard's ranch but she was only now regaining full consciousness. She was stretched out on a blanket under an overhang of rock and Gideon cradled her head and gave her a drink from his canteen. She spluttered and coughed, but grabbed instinctively at the water-bottle and drank a couple of deep gulps, rubbing her bruised jaw gently.

Then she opened her eyes and stared up at him for a couple of minutes before suddenly blinking, then starting to push up on her elbows.

'Wha. . . ? Where am I. . . ? Clay. . . ?'

Gideon nodded in the growing light as the first rays of sunlight fanned over the Moonlight Range.

'Just take it easy, Bobbie. You've had a rough night.' He half-smiled.

Memory must have flooded in because she looked shocked, her face coloured deeply and she struggled to a sitting posiiton, trying to hold the bodice of her low-cut, short-skirted dress so as to hide her cleavage.

'A little late,' Gideon said, slightly amused. 'I hardly recognized you sitting in Coke's lap—'

'Oh, damn you!' she flared. 'It's not funny! My jaw aches and feels like it's broken!'

'You wouldn't be able to cuss me if it was. Bobbie, I think you owe us an explanation. . . .'

136

She glared at all three of them and then seemed to calm down and her embarrassment hit her again. She fiddled with the dress, then sighed. She told them about the spontaneous idea that had occurred to her when she had found the stranded whores on the trail to Graveyard.

'I thought Blanchard might just kick me off once he knew I was a lawyer working on your behalf, Clay. So, it occurred to me that if he thought I was just a . . . good-time girl I might be able to take a look around for myself or – at worst – wheedle some information out of him before . . . before he discovered . . . differently.'

Buckskin snorted.

'Ma'am, you took a mighty risk. Bull Blanchard likes to treat his women rough and you wouldn'ta had much chance to . . . play with him before he decided to . . . take what he wanted. . . .'

Her eyes widened. 'You mean. . . ?'

Buckskin felt a little embarrassed himself now and nodded curtly, looking as if he wished he hadn't opened his mouth. Gideon, trying to save Bobbie any further discomfort, told her how the Indian had started the fires so as to give them a chance to escape from Coke and the others.

'Well. Where are we?' She looked around bewilderedly.

'On my land. Near the creek. I want to take a look at the gold diggings, and see how far Bull's tunnel goes under my land.'

'Good!' she said instantly, getting to her feet and seeming to forget about the skimpy outfit she wore.

'That's what I wanted to do, too, but I wasn't sure how I could accomplish it. Can we do it now?'

Gideon hesitated.

'Getting light fast, Clay,' said the Indian.

Gideon nodded. 'Yeah. Bull'll have men looking for us by now and he might think about the tunnel. Can you handle a gun?'

He addressed this last to Roberta McHugh and she smiled slightly, reached somewhere into a complex fold of the short skirt and drew out a small, four-barrelled pepperbox pistol, a Sharps Model in .30 calibre rimfire. It weighed no more than ten ounces and was only adequate for close work.

'I call this my 'special' gun. I can shoot the pip out of an ace of spades at ten paces with it.'

And that's about as accurate as the damn thing would ever get, Gideon thought.

But what puzzled him was: where did she learn to shoot like that? And why was it 'special'?

CHAPTER 12

GRAVEYARD

Bull was still trying to whip up some enthusiasm in his crew when Abe Chance rode in with half a dozen posse men.

Blanchard stood near the charred porch, six-gun strapped on, his rifle and a box of ammunition in his hands.

Abe rode his lathered horse across, trying to soothe it by patting its slippery neck.

'Been doin' some hard riding,' Blanchard observed, deadpan.

'Not as hard as I figure to do.' The sheriff jerked his head at the house and the other fire-scarred buildings. 'I see he got this far.'

Bull stiffened. 'Who got this far?'

'That goddamned Gideon! With his Injun pard and that old polecat Buckskin. They nigh burned the town out!'

'*That's* who it was! Hell, we figured Injuns because of the fire arrows but I thought Gideon was still locked up in jail.'

There was accusation in his hot glare.

'Yeah, well, that damn Injun rained fire arrows down on the town, started six or seven fires all round the place – store, livery and so on. We *had* to fight 'em. While we was doin' that someone broke Gideon out. Likely Buckskin.'

Bull swore briefly.

'Then he's somewhere on the loose out here – on my land!'

'Yeah, but I know where you'll find him.'

He waited for Bull's reaction, got it in the surprised stare and then the impatient growl.

'Well, where, for Chris'sakes! It's near daylight now. . . .'

'Pete Dane tried to stop 'em and got hisself shot. He'll likely pull through but he told me he heard Gideon say he was gonna check on your diggin's – for the gold.'

He lowered his voice on the last three words and Blanchard's face tightened.

'*Right!*' he said, and swung away towards the horses his exhausted men had readied for the trail. 'Let's go, men!'

Abe grabbed the rancher's arm, and Bull swung back, angry with impatience. The sheriff spoke in a low voice.

'Bull, we got townsmen here. They didn't want to come, some've got damage to their houses or businesses. Best if we don't let 'em know about the gold. How about I send 'em back, tell 'em we've got enough men usin' yours?'

'Yeah, well, they're a sorry bunch,' Bull growled

looking at his hangdog, begrimed crew, 'but sounds like a good idea. Just hope it don't come to a stand-up, eye-to-eye gunfight. Don't reckon any of 'em'd be worth a ruptured squirrel.'

But that's what they did, sent the townsmen back, and they were mighty pleased to go, were gone out of the yard in a cloud of dust, with a whoop and holler, before the sheriff had finished speaking.

The remainder who made up the rag-tag posse moved off in the direction of the gold diggings on the broken, blasted face of the mountain where the slim waterfall had once flowed, but which was now the lid on the giant coffin that held the bodies of the Dutch family Vermeer.

No one except Blanchard and Chance seemed in any way enthusiastic.

'No wonder we never saw 'em working,' Clay Gideon said, sitting his saddle and looking at the scarred face of the mountain, still bearing some of the blackened scars of the explosion that had brought down tons of rock and earth. 'It's on the side away from Lazy G. We had the whole damn mountain between us.'

There were several piles of mullock, wheeled out of the mine on the battered wooden barrows which were tipped on their sides or standing up against rocks or the mullock slopes. They must have blasted at least part of the way in, and the entrance had been shored up with heavy, though green, timber: logs cut from living trees and jammed in under the cavelike mine entrance, jutting out overhead slightly.

They tethered their horses amongst the rocks, out

of sight unless anyone was really looking for them. They half-expected guards but it was obvious that Bull had done all the work on this part he intended to do.

The entrance ran in for maybe fifty feet, then veered left towards the creek, beginning to angle down.

'Must've moved half the mountain,' opined Buckskin, stooping. The shaft was barely high enough for a grown man to stand in although Roberta had no trouble.

She had unpinned the dress that had exposed the long white length of one leg to just above the knee, wiped off most of the paint and rouge on her face and let down her hair to fan about her shoulders. She looked a little different from when she had first arrived, for then she had had the hair caught in a chignon, but it was loose now and she no longer resembled a 'soiled dove'.

There was still a little gold-bearing quartz glittering in the light of the oil-lamps they had found stacked inside the mine entrance.

Gideon pointed to the thin snakelike quartz veins.

'In a hurry. Not bothering with the small stuff.'

'Why would he think it led to a big lode?' Roberta asked.

Gideon shrugged. 'Remember hearing that Bull worked in the California gold rush. Guess he knows something about gold-mining.'

'I better stay here and keep an eye on things,' Buckskin said suddenly, hefting his battered old Sharps. Gideon looked at him and Buck added, slightly embarrassed: 'Fact is I ain't easy underground. Figure I'll be there soon enough without any trial runs.'

Gideon smiled thinly.

'Keep your eyes open, Buck, Bull will be along sooner or later.'

He turned to the Indian. 'You want to come or stay?'

'I'll come,' said the Indian although he didn't seem very comfortable with the idea.

'Then let's go. See if we can get some notion of where he crosses into my land and for how far.'

Roberta hesitated. 'It – seems to slope down again.'

There was a slight breathlessness when she spoke and Gideon glanced at her sharply.

'You want to stay with Buck, it's OK, Bobbie.'

She hesitated, then shook her head, lips firming slightly.

'No, I'll come. I want to see how close he is to realizing his dream.' Clay frowned and let his gaze linger on her but she smiled briefly and gestured into the darkness that awaited them. 'I'll follow. The Indian can follow me.'

That was how they moved on, feeling the broken slope begin to steepen. They could see, when they held the lanterns close to the gouged walls, where the Graveyard crew had prised out thin lines of gold-bearing quartz. There was the smell of dank earth and the overlying pungency of explosives.

Then they came upon a small stack of boxes of dynamite with charges, all fused and with detonators. Gideon studied the walls and then lifted his lantern towards the ceiling. There were traces of sand showing amongst the rocks that looked more like pebbles than jagged-layered shale and quartz.

'I think we're under the creek here,' he said quietly

and he saw the girl's eyes widen. The Indian's face was impassive as usual. 'Guess they weren't going to do any blasting around here. They'd use the pickaxes and crowbars to dig the tunnel yonder.' As he spoke he moved across to the dark maw of the tunnel where it dog-legged slightly. His light showed the unmistakable marks of pickaxe blades and crowbars and cold chisels.

'Why – why wouldn't they blast?' asked Roberta tensely.

'Under the creek like I said. It's the dry part but they wouldn't risk it caving in – if it did, it might collapse all the way back to where the water is pooled and this tunnel would be flooded.'

'My God! We could drown!'

'Take it easy.' We're not going to be doing any blasting.' He wanted to get the girl's mind off being buried alive or drowned down here and waved his lantern. 'I'd say they're a good thirty-five feet into my land – and they still haven't hit the lode. It could be another two feet or a hundred, but the fact that they're taking gold from my land ought to put them on the wrong side of the law, right?'

He saw the way she had to wrench her mind back to the legal problem and knew she was thinking of a tunnel collapse and the disaster that would follow.

'We-ell – er, yes! Yes, it would constitute theft because the very fact that the line of the creek is so . . . obvious.' She gestured to the section of roof where the gritty sand and pebblelike rocks showed amongst the quartz and shale. 'It makes it clear where the boundary is and if Blanchard kept digging, as he has, then he is stealing gold that is rightfully yours.'

144

'Then we've got him.'

'Clay, he's breaking the law, but to say we've "got" him – well, this is Blanchard's stamping-ground and you know he has the backing of Judge Galbally and Sheriff Chance!'

'Sure. But here's the evidence – all around us!'

'Yes, it's here *now*, but once we charge Blanchard with theft, how long do you think it would stay here?'

Gideon shook his head. 'I know Bull well enough to figure he wouldn't blow it down to cover it up, not when he thinks he's so close to the big lode.'

'He'll kill you instead,' the Indian said flatly and the words seemed to echo loudly and hang in the still, silent air of the tomblike tunnel.

Roberta nodded solemnly.

'Sure,' said Gideon. 'He'll try. But if your man got through to Durango and the Governor sends down the army we can . . .'

He broke off at the sound of a heavy gunshot slapping flatly through the underground tunnel.

'Buckskin,' the Indian said quietly and Gideon turned and began to run, crouching, back the way they had come. He turned his head briefly to call to the Indian.

'Bring her with you! But stay back until we see what's going on.'

Roberta felt the Indian's big, blunt-fingered hand reach for her and then she was being dragged back up the slope of the tunnel.

A volley of distant gunfire reached her dully.

Buckskin's first shot blew a Graveyard rider clear out

of the saddle, the man's body somersaulting through the air, cannoning off a tree before falling to the ground where it lay very still.

The men scattered, including Bull Blanchard and Abe Chance. They sought cover amongst the rocks and a few trees, the echoes of the Sharps still pulsing through the early morning.

Bull had his rifle in his hand, looking at the mouth of the mine. Some powdersmoke curled out and was tattered by the breeze that drifted across the land at this time of day.

'He ain't far inside.'

' 'Course not,' growled the sheriff, squinting. 'He couldn't see us properly if he was too far back. Gonna be a real son of a bitchin' job to get by that buffalo-gun.'

Bull nodded and then looked at Coke who was dismounted, crouched by a rock, pistol in hand.

'You never did like that smelly old bastard, did you, Coke?'

Coke glanced over his shoulder, frowning, searching for the meaning in Bull's words.

'Never did.' He spat. 'You want me to go down and blow him out from under that coonskin hat?'

Bull smiled crookedly.

'Be worth a hundred bucks.'

'On my way.'

As Coke moved off, doubled over, making his way through the rocks, Abe said:

'Rather him than me. Just look at what one of them slugs did to your man! Blew him wide open.'

'Coke's good. He used to slip up behind Reb sentries and cut their throats or rip their kidneys out.

If anyone can get to that mountain man, it's him.'

Abe pursed his lips, still not convinced.

But Coke was as good as Bull said; he had been the top sentry-killer of Bannister's Troop. It was the basis of Colonel Bannister's success: send in Coke to clear the way, then move in silently with deadly, ruthless precision on the Confederate positions and, later, wipe out any nearby families on the assumption that they had aided the Rebs.

Coke hadn't forgotten a thing about those bloody days and nights when Bannister's patrols wandered all through the South, leaving a trail of dead men, and sometimes women and children, behind.

He climbed up the broken face of the hillside as Buckskin began shooting again, picking off the horses he could see, the animals going down with barely a sound, the heavy slugs were so deadly and accurate. The Graveyard men poured lead into the mine shaft at Bull's instructions, forcing Buckskin to keep his head down. This gave Coke his chance to clamber across the face of the slope right above the entrance, gun in his holster now.

He moved carefully, hoping his *compadres* would keep their shots low; it would be ironic if one of them shot him off the side of the mountain before he could get to Buckskin. But he placed his boots so they didn't dislodge any loose stones, took his weight on whitened, straining fingertips, at least one nail tearing loose from his left index finger.

He bit back against the pain, feeling the blood flow as he reached out with his long left leg, searching for

147

and finding a secure foothold and shifting his weight
warily. He jumped when the Sharps bellowed just
below him and tried not to cough in the raw powdersmoke that rose out of the tunnel mouth where he
was crouching on one of the big green bracing-logs.

Leaning out carefully, hat hanging down his back
by its tie thong, he saw Buckskin reloading, heard the
breech clash closed on a fresh cartridge, the tinkle of
the ejected empty case. Holding tight as he could
with his blood-slippery left hand to a projecting rock,
he swung his body slightly down so he could see
better past the log.

Buckskin caught his movement on his peripheral
vision, and the oldster moved faster than he had for
years. He threw himself backwards, angling the
Sharps up, the butt braced into his skinny hip. The
buffalo-gun thundered and dirt and stones and a
handful of greenwood splinters exploded from the
top of the shaft entrance. Coke let out a yell as he
fell, arms flailing.

But he had managed to get off his shot and when
he landed, winded, struggling to get to all fours, he
saw Buck was down, writhing, blood splashed on the
front of his buckskin shirt. Coke grinned as he
fought to his hands and knees, his face straightening
fast when he saw Buck struggling and fumbling to get
another shell into the hot breech. It froze Coke in a
moment of terror, and then he saw movement
behind Buck and stumbled, putting down his
gunhand to steady himself as Clay Gideon came
running out of the darkness of the mine, shooting
from the hip.

Coke staggered as a slug found his body but he brought his gun around across his belly, triggering. He missed and Gideon's gun jammed or he had lost a percussion cap, but he didn't waste any time trying to correct the misfire.

He dropped the Remington pistol and launched himself bodily across the wounded Buckskin, snatching the Sharps from the fumbling old hands, closing the breech and firing as he landed with a jolt. Afterwards, he wasn't sure whether it was the impact of landing that jarred him so much or the recoil kick from the big rifle.

Not that it mattered. Coke was picked up by the massive slug and his body hurtled several feet, broken and spraying blood. Ears ringing, Gideon scrambled back into the dimness and the slender safety afforded by the passage, wriggling over towards Buck. The oldster was making gagging sounds and he curled up, bony knees almost against his chest, old eyes seeking Gideon. As Clay knelt by him, ducking a little as guns rattled outside and raked the mine entrance, he heard someone coming out of the tunnel. It was Roberta, and she was alone.

'Where's the Indian?'

'I – I don't know; he just told me to keep going until I found you. He went back for something. . . .'

She crouched against the wall, wincing as two bullets ricocheted from the walls. They heard Bull's voice outside:

'That's it! Shoot in at an angle! Bounce your bullets off the wall!'

Gideon hunkered down closer, felt for Buckskin's

149

heart beat. It barely pulsed against his seeking fingers. He looked down into the old man's gaunted face, the eyes staring up at him gradually losing their lustre. A hand clawed at him, held his shirt-sleeve, drawing him close. But if Buckskin had anything to say it was drowned by the gunfire from outside and the zip and drone of ricocheting bullets.

Then the old man fell back, limp.

'*Adios, compadre,*' Gideon said quietly, reaching for the Sharps again. 'See if you can find another shell,' he said to the girl.

Then the Indian came in a crouching run out of the tunnel's blackness, a firefly keeping him company. Then the firefly rose from his side, up near his shoulder and it was launched from the tunnel mouth into the rocks beyond. Gideon watched the thin trail of smoke curving up and then down towards the rocks where the shooting had come from.

The dynamite exploded in an eruption of dirt and stones and shattered rock. By then the Indian had a second fuse burning and he threw this stick as well. But as he turned away from the entrance, he staggered, went down to one knee with a coughing grunt.

'You hit?' called Gideon, but his words were drowned by the blast of the second stick of dynamite.

He crawled to the Indian who told him he was OK.

'But we better get out of here,' he added breathlessly. 'I set a box to explode. Figured if we were goners, then at least Blanchard wouldn't get the gold.'

'Good thinking, but it'll likely blow through the creek bottom and—'

'That's why we have to get – out – *Now*!'

150

The second blast had torn out trees and brush and Bull's surviving crew were riding out hell for leather, away from the mine and the broken mountain. Through the ringing in his ears, Gideon could hear Blanchard shouting after them.

Then the girl handed Gideon another Sharps cartridge and he slammed it home, triggered towards the sound of the voice. The bullet ricocheted with a sound like a dozen hornets. Bull Blanchard and Abe Chance figured things had gone mighty bad on them and seconds later were spurring their mounts away after their men.

Gideon knew he had to leave Buck where he was. there wasn't time to take him. He grabbed the girl and dragged her out of the mine as the Indian stumbled through the entrance, left hand pressed against his side. Gideon slowed some when he saw the size of the blood-patch but the Indian waved him on irritably and they made it to where they had stashed the horses. The girl took Buck's mount – she had ridden double with Clay on the way up – and Gideon led the way out, seeing the Indian was doubled over his mount's neck, just hanging on.

Behind them, the mountain trembled and the rising ground shook beneath their horses' hoofs, making the animals whinny and shudder and swerve. The girl cried out in alarm as her mount almost slithered out from under her but it regained its footing and continued to carry her up and over the mountain.

'Might as well make for my place,' Gideon called, frowning as he saw the Indian was having trouble

151

holding on, his blood splashing on to his mount's withers now.

He reined around and went back, gesturing to the girl to keep going. 'Turn by a tall boulder. Candlerock. It's downhill all the way then.'

He leaned from the saddle to steady the Indian. The man turned his head and Gideon saw his face. Blood ran from his mouth and his eyes blazed with a fierce intensity that Clay knew came just before life would begin to fade.

'We should get across to Lazy G before stopping,' he said and the Indian nodded that he could make it.

With Gideon riding close, holding the doubled-over Indian in the saddle, they made the climb, turned at Candlerock and began the descent.

Bull Blanchard reined down on a rise to look back and Abe slid to a halt beside him. They saw the smoke and dust still curling out of the mineshaft, or what remained of it.

It had collapsed and even now rocks were sliding down the broken face of the mountain, piling up where the tunnel entrance had been. He swore and looked beyond, standing in the stirrups so he could see the creek.

'God almighty!' he breathed, pointing, unable to say more right away.

Abe stood in his stirrups, too, saw the creek as no one had ever seen it before. The narrow bend which had been virtually dry, with bare inches of muddied water linking it and the main pools above and below, was now a large crater, some of the sides still tumbling inwards. Water flowed from the deep pools upstream, eroding the banks as it gathered momentum, pouring down into the crater and below into the tunnel that had been dug below. The whole roof had collapsed with the dynamite blast, sucked in the cataract of roaring creek water, flooding the shafts, filling them not only with water but with boulders and tons of earth and tree trunks, sealing the mineface where the lode was thought to be for ever.

'The bastard!' Bull screamed to the smoke-and-dirt-smudged sky. Trembling, eyes bulging he turned to Abe Chance. 'He's won! The – son – of – a –bitch – has – won!'

Chance's face hardened, his mouth a tight razor slash.

'Not yet!' He pointed to the three riders making their way around the mountain to the trail that led to Gideon's land. 'They might've stopped us gettin' that gold, but it don't mean they gotta live to enjoy it!'

'No, by Christ!' Blanchard gritted, already spurring his weary mount across the slope. 'If it's the last thing I do, I'm gonna see Clay Gideon dead!'

'If I get to him first, that's just how you'll find him. Hell, I don't even care if he nails me, too! Long as I get him!'

The Indian couldn't make it any further.

They came down from the slopes on to Gideon's Lazy G but the wounded Navajo couldn't hold on any longer. Gideon strained to keep him in the saddle but it was useless. The man was too heavy and slack now.

The Indian spilled from the horse, bounced several

times, came to rest against a deadfall. The girl was already hauling rein but Gideon leapt from his mount without bothering to stop it, stumbling and skidding as he fought to halt his momentum so he could get back to the Indian.

He knelt and when he turned the man over he saw the wound was much worse than the Indian had let on. Splintered ribs were showing and purple-red torn flesh which he knew must be a lung.

'Sorry, Indian.'

'I know it is my time, *amigo.*' His voice was raspy but he seemed lucid enough. 'You know the canyon of pueblos. My family is buried there – beneath the Wall of the Spirits. You will know this by – by the – rock paintings – men, animals, symbols of the Endless Circle of Life. . . .'

Gideon started to frown but stopped and nodded.

'I'll find it – but – why?'

'You – will bury me – there, Clay? With my – family – I am the – last. . . .'

Gideon hesitated briefly, nodded.

'If I survive, I'll do it.'

The Indian started to rise, was too weak. Gideon leaned down when he saw the man wanted to say something.

In a hoarse whisper, the Indian said:

'I am Laki-Il-Ho-ney. Say my name – with the last handful of – dust so the – Great Spirit may know – I – am – coming. . . .'

'Laki-Il-Ho-ney,' repeated Gideon solemnly.

'Next to my – mother.' The Indian was gasping now, trying to hold on these last few seconds, to give

154

Gideon his final instructions. 'She – was of the Medicine Clan – she could make a wind come – on a still day – call an eagle to – guard our – house from – snakes – she – she . . .'

He said something in a language Gideon didn't understand, managed a couple of words of his personal Death Song, then coughed in a heavy spasm, and fell back with eyes open, though dulled in death.

Gideon closed them and the girl, white-faced and obviously upset said:

'Clay. They're coming!'

Gideon realized he had been concentrating on the Indian and hadn't heard the horses. Abe Chance and Bull Blanchard were coming down the slope on foot, faces set for vengeance. Clay hit the girl in the back of the legs and she cried out in surprise as she fell. He pushed her in behind the deadfall near the Indian, pulled his Remington out and triggered. It misfired again and he remembered he hadn't checked the percussion caps since the mine.

Bullets kicked splinters into his face as he pulled the pin and dropped out the cylinder, reaching into his belt pouch for the spare which was fully loaded with percussion caps already in place on the nipples. He pinned it back, spun the first cap beneath the hammer and reached over the log, triggering.

Abe Chance was kneeling on a rock so he could see over the deadfall, rifle to his shoulder. He slid off the rock and hit the ground running, yelling crazily as he charged at Gideon, levering and triggering. His motion set the bullets flying all over the landscape and Gideon threw himself aside and fired while still in mid-air. The slug went close, didn't hit, but was enough to make Abe stumble and he twisted, teeth bared in his effort to line up the rifle on Gideon.

Clay beaded him coldly and triggered, thumbing the hammer again, putting a second ball into the man even as he toppled. It spun the sheriff around and the man skidded down on his back, his face masked with blood, eyes staring. But he was dead and never felt the sickening crunch as his skull splintered against the deadfall.

Gideon wheeled towards Bull, having lost sight of Blanchard while he was trading lead with Chance. He was surprised to see the man standing at the far end of the deadfall, panting and sweating, but his rifle was steady enough as he covered Gideon and the girl crouched beside him.

'Well, at least I get the pleasure of watching my bullet go into you, Gideon!' He jerked the rifle barrel. 'Get up – slow, and with your hands empty.'

As Clay obeyed Blanchard looked down at the still crouched girl.

'You, too, lady. Say, I've seen you before!' There was sharp interest in his face and tone now. Then utter surprise spread across his dirt-grimed features. 'By Godfrey! You're the one shot Bannister! Walked right up to him, said somethin' and put a bullet between his eyes!'

Gideon snapped his gaze to Roberta as she stared and slowly began to rise. He could see her right hand where he was, although Bull Blanchard couldn't. It went into the folds of her skirt.

'You're right, Bull!' she said, as she straightened

out. 'I told Bannister I'd been on my way to marry Hans Vermeer when he and his bunch of murderers slaughtered the whole family close to here – because they'd given a gun to a fugitive Johnny Reb.' She glanced at Gideon and then brought up the Sharps pepperbox and fired point black into Blanchard's face.

He went over backwards without a sound, the .30 calibre ball smashing between his eyes.

She let the gun fall and sat down on the deadfall, trembling, but showing no other signs of distress. Gideon sat down beside her, waiting until she was ready to speak.

'I was betrothed to Hans Vermeer. He was badly wounded in a Yankee raid, lost both his legs, and they let him return to his family. Crippled or not, I wanted to marry him, but before I could reach the Vermeer ranch . . .'

'Bannister and Blanchard wiped the whole family out. You know it was me they gave the rifle to?'

'Yes. I set out to track down that Yankee group and kill them one by one. When I finished my legal training I used all our research facilities and was preparing to come after Blanchard, the last one, when your wife came to our firm with her story. It was just what I needed to get close to Blanchard without his suspecting anything.' She smiled quite coldly. 'I planned to destroy his chances of getting that gold, if the big lode did in fact exist – whether it did or not didn't matter. He *believed* it did and would be devastated if he was prevented from getting it just as he thought he had his hands on a fortune.'

Gideon digested what she had said, studied her silently.

'Just to look at you, no one would ever think you could be so cold-blooded, Bobbie.'

She shrugged. 'I feel – drained now. But – satisfied. I have you and your wife to thank for that, Clay.' She indicated the gun in the dust. 'And that, of course. Hans gave it to me – for my protection while he was away at the war. . . .'

She looked pensive and Gideon was at a loss what to say when they heard the sound of many horses coming. Clay reached for his gun but she stayed his hand as an army troop rode up, a captain in the lead. He threw them a salute. Threw *Roberta* a salute, anyway.

'Bobbie, I'm mighty glad to see you alive and well. Though I recollect I've seen you dressed somewhat better.'

'Captain Martin Hawkins. Your presence is a surprise. Am I to take it that Hush delivered my papers to the Governor?'

'Yes, ma'am. But he was badly wounded, just made it to Durango. Oh, he'll live, according to our sawbones, but he refused all treatment until he had given the Governor those papers of yours. This, I take it, is Clay Gideon who will, I am sure, explain these dead man and the general chaos and destruction we passed on the mountain.'

'I'm Gideon and this is my land. I'll be glad to explain, Captain, but I best tell you that I still have a powerful enemy in Bannister Springs, named Judge Galbally.'

Hawkins lifted a hand, shaking his head.

'Not so, Gideon. The judge is on his way – in hand-cuffs – to Durango under escort to make his own explanations to the Governor. I've a feeling they won't be very satisfactory so I think you won't be seeing him again – unless you attend the court proceedings in Denver next month. Now, for *your* explanation. . . .'

Gideon was near exhausted after he had finished and the captain had his cook make strong coffee for all. Gideon drank his sitting on a rock away from the others and Roberta McHugh came across, holding her own tin mug of java.

'Captain Hawkins said it's a little complicated but he believes you won't be charged with anything too serious. You were provoked and the Governor is very strong on keeping relations between the North and South on a much more friendly and co-operative footing than it has been. Martin will allow you to bury your Indian friend if you want, but you must give him your word you will come to Durango and report to him afterwards.'

Gideon looked steadily at her.

'You going to back me up?'

She hesitated, then said: 'I said I would be respon-sible for you keeping your word, yes. . . .'

'Thanks, Bobbie. I'll look you up in Denver.'

'You'll be coming there?'

'Sure. That's where Lanie is, isn't she? And we've got a lot of time to make up.'

'Yes, of course.' She hesitated, mildly uncomfortable. 'Clay, I know Lanie wants to come back to you but – well, I'm not sure she wants to come back *here* – to Lazy G, I mean.'

'Yeah, well, that's something we'll have to work out but at least we can do it face to face.'

Roberta nodded slowly and drank from her coffee-mug. 'I hope it works out for you, Clay.'

He stood, smiled quickly, then arched his back trying to take some of the kinks out of it. He looked away to the distant Moonlights, seeing beyond them to the land of the pueblos and the secret canyon where he would lay the Indian to rest.

When he got there on a still, stifling day, the Indian's body wrapped in a blanket on a travois, he found the Wall of the Spirits with the faded ochre paintings and the smudged marks of prayer fires around the base.

He buried the Indian in the hard red earth and as he sprinkled the last handful of red dust on the grave mound he said aloud,

'Great Spirit, Laki-Il-Ho-ney has come home.'

He felt a little self-conscious but then a coldness ran through him as he turned away and in that still-ness where there was no wind, no perceptible stirring of the air, a small red swirl of dust rose from the grave mound and momentarily enveloped him.

He always thought of it afterwards as the Indian's last farewell.